For

As Long As the Skies Exist

For As Long As the Skies Exist

Kavita Padgaonkar Ajmera

MANJUL
Manjul Publishing House Pvt. Ltd.

First published in India by

MANJUL

Manjul Publishing House Pvt. Ltd.,
10, Nishat Colony, Bhopal, INDIA-462 003
Ph.: 91-755-4240340, Fax : 91-755-2736919
E-mail : manjul@manjulindia.com
Website : www.manjulindia.com

First published : 2008

ISBN 978 - 81 - 8322 - 108 - 5

Printed and bound in India by
Gopsons Papers Ltd.

Acknowledgement

The credit for writing this story in the goes first to the inventor of the PC, and my resultant desire of to type effortlessly on he keyboard, and thereafter to the belief that there is a story in each of us. I just had to know my story.

Writing a story, difficult as it may seem, is the easy part. To see friends and family enraptured by it is exhilarating, gratifying and satisfying at the same time. But to have a friend believe in your story so completely, that he makes it his life's purpose to see it culminate into a book, is humbling. I begin, therefore, by first thanking my colleague, Dr. Ajay Kakar, who has been so generous with his time and encouragement and without whom this book would perhaps have remained a manuscript on my laptop. Thank you Ajay, this book is as mch a labour of love for you as if for me.

I would also like to especially thank :

My husband Himanshu, whose persona defines the manifold aspects of love and who over the wonderful years that we have been together, had become my Aakash, 'my piece of heaven.'

My children Hitesh and Krish, who've enthralled me with the roller coaster ride called motherhood. Of all my identities, I really enjoy being 'mommy' the most.

All my friends and family, who read the story and gave insightful inputs to make this book complete, I pray that love, like it is found in this book, is yours.

My Father, the late Anil Padgaonkar, mother Dr. Asha Padgaonkar, sister Dr. Devika Gupta, all my loves and infatuations and all of the above mentioned - I owe gratitude, for it is from them that I have learnt what love should and should not be.

Artist Kanchanmala Ghosh for helping me with the sketches that complement my poems.

Padma Shree Professor P. Lal and his Writer's Workshop, for being the first to endorse my work, thereby giving it life.

Dr. Rumpa Wig, to whom I shall always remain indebted for putting this story in the able hands of Manjul Publishing House.

Manjul Publishing House, for believing in this first time another. Especially Manoj Kulkarni for his kind and gentle handling of the book and its authoress.

Saving the best for the last, my gratitued to that energy which is bigger than all of us. The energy that guides us, is us, and which, in its most complex or simple form, we call love - I salute thee.

The Author

Kavita Padgaonkar Ajmera is a practising dentist in Kolkata. She was born in Mumbai, India, but spent the better part of her childhood in New Delhi and completed high school at Loreto Convent, Delhi Cantt. She was actively involved in school sports, drama and elocution and was the Head Prefect in her final year at school. She went to Indore to take a Bachelor's degree in Science. It is during this time that she started writing poems. Returning to Kolkata, where her parents were residing, she discovered another passion - golf. After pursuing the game wholeheartedly for two years she decided to become a dentist, a dream she had pursued ever since she had walked into a dental clinic as a child. With a satisfying and successful dental career in her bag and her children now at university, writing is her newest love. *For As Long As The Skies Exist* is her maiden publication.

About the Book

"All she wanted was a virtual friend she could talk to and who would appreciate her for herself, not for being Mrs Rahul Sud."

Amrita and Aakash meet on the net and fall deeply in love. The two spend a romantic day together but being realistic and practical, they part ways and go back from their dream to the real world with the hope that they meet will again but with the knowledge that they never will.

The story takes a turn when Amrita realizes that she is pregnant with Aakash's child. She decides to keep the baby, for it is a precious part of Aakash, but vows not to involve him at all as he has moved to the USA to find a new life. Single-handedly, she takes care of her daughters, the twins Rhea and Alia, and Aakash's child Aasma, as well as her ailing husband and the flourishing Sud empire. Fate plays it's own game when time and again Aakash comes into Amrita's life and she finds herself going through an emotional and psychological catharsis.

This is a story for those who believe that the sky is the limit for the power of love, and that love lives for a long, long time - at least for as long as the skies exist.

Dedication

For the three most important men in my life - Himanshu, Hitesh and Krish.

CHAPTER 1

An Ode To Life

Sounds of silence and deep reflections,
I delve into my being.
Life has been a growing up job,
But not always upstream.

Life, you gave me pain,
Pain - so I could see joy.
Life, you kept me alone sometimes,
So much that I wanted to die.

But die you taught me was the easy part,
You gave me courage to smile.
To find the strength within my heart,
To walk the extra mile.

To find at the end of the road,
Friends with love in their souls.
To find that love is not easily got,
I must learn to love with no hold.

Freedom is the key word,
That's the way we came.
Bound by norms and emotions,
We lose our place in the frame.

Kavita Padgaonkar Ajmera

In the picture painted for each of us
When good times were hard to come by,
You taught me life that fences can stop
Only those who cannot fly.

What is life if not deep friendship?
What is friendship if not sweet love?
What is love if not a journey,
To know there's a God above?

And God will call on me one day,
Take me back to life with Him.
The consummation of life will then be complete,
And my 'Ode to Love' begin.

Amrita sighed deeply, shut her diary and stood staring mindlessly at the sprawling and tastefully landscaped lawn. The lemon chiffon sari worn with a matching sleeveless blouse accentuated her delicate frame and also her grief. Leaning against the large glass and mahogany window that occupied the entire span of the wall, she reveled in the beauty of the lusciously green lawn and carefully manicured flowerbeds. Bonsais and seasonal flowers along with a riot of ferns made for a colourful canvas. She couldn't help comparing her life to this garden of her creation.

She had every thing that most women craved; just like the beautiful garden with all its fancy trimmings. Unlike the garden though, hers was a life devoid of an essential aroma. The aroma emitted by the tender, loving care of the keeper - that of complete and unconditional love. Loneliness and the void that the past few years had created were compounded by the fact that she had to swallow her pride and live the farce that her life had become. For the sake of her young daughters, that was something she just had to come to terms with whether she liked it or not. She was depressed and felt very alone.

Amrita determinedly walked away from the window and sat in front of the computer. The July afternoon heat was killing, but comfortably ensconced in her airconditioned study she switched on her computer and logged on to the 'Internet chat'. Rahul was on one of his never-ending tours and the need for company was compelling. Normally a shy and demure housewife, Amrita would never have dared to seek out male company in real life or even on the net for that matter. There was the image to think about and if word ever got out that she was on the prowl - heaven forbid! There was no guessing what barriers Rahul's temper could breach. God knew her daughters were far too precious for her to take any chances with it. She had kept secret the torture he bestowed on her all these years and ignored the vacuum that was tugging at her mental and physical self. Virtual friends were fun and entertaining, she had heard at the kitty party. One's identity remained discreet and so no one was the wiser for it. She wasn't looking for 'relationships' like the ones those women spoke of. All she wanted was a friend she could talk to and who would appreciate her for herself, not for being Mrs. Rahul Sud. Most of all, a friend who would not take their conversations back to Rahul. A male friend - because she needed the excitement too!

Rahul was a jetsetting business tycoon. He spoke only in millions and had a lifestyle to match. A home that was the envy of many, plush offices all over the country and abroad and of course : there was Gayatri. A successful man's prerogative - his friends called her. Rahul would laugh it off and insist she was only his PR officer who just had to travel with him on work. For Amrita, Gayatri was now nothing but a numb reality. She had resigned herself to Rahul's dominance and played the part of wife and mother to the hilt. She didn't have a choice.

Life carried on, the monotonous kitty parties which she had to be a part of being Mrs. Rahul Sud, the charitable organizations on whose board meetings she was the silent pretty face, the mandatory shopping to keep the image. All so futile and materialistic, so unlike the person she was when Rahul had married her.

Amrita was the daughter of Brig. S.J. Bakshi. She had lived the life that any service family does. Hoping one day to realize her dream of becoming an ace architect, she relentlessly pursued academics. It was during her second year in college that she had met Rahul, or rather Rahul had met her. For Rahul the beautiful, intelligent and elusive Amrita was a challenge, and challenges he loved. The Bakshis were delighted with such a grand proposal and there was little Amrita could do against such strong parental pressure. She was promptly married off to Rahul; and life, as she had hoped for, ceased to exist.

Marriage at first took a lot of adjusting, but Rahul was the doting and indulgent husband and Amrita soon fit into the groove of things. The ongoing years witnessed the births of her twins, Alia and Rhea and also the growth of the Sud Empire. That's when life changed once again. Amrita was confronted with having to cope with an entire new set of rules that had been laid down by Rahul. Rules that were never spoken of by him, but were amply understood by her. She had made her peace with destiny but was never again at peace with herself.

The words on the screen leapt at her and shook her out of her reverie.

"asl?"

"EXCUSE ME?" she replied.

"Are you new to chatting?"

"VERY NEW." She replied honestly.

"No wonder you didn't understand what I asked. OK, I'll write in regular type for you. Btw- that's 'by the way' for you, don't use capitals, in chat parlance it suggests shouting. You didn't know that, did you?"

"NO, oops! I mean no I did not know that. Thank you." She typed.

"Hmm, well-mannered too. Let's start the introductions again, shall we?"

"OK."

"Hi, I'm Aakash. Age, sex and location please asl - get it?"

He had introduced himself and his conduct gave her good vibes. Amrita decided to honour the chat request.

"I am a twenty-nine year old married woman, does it matter where I live?"

"Lol, no not at all, but I don't want to be chatting with my next door neighbour's wife, or worse still his fifteen year old daughter, lol. L.O.L. is the abbreviation for 'laughing out loud'. Btw- remember that one?"

"Yes, I know that now and what you mean too," she liked his forthrightness, "I am in Delhi, and you? Tell me about yourself."

"That's a relief then, if you really are in Delhi, that is. I see no reason to doubt you; though with this medium we can't ever be sure, can we? Anyway, I am in Jammu and that is the truth."

"Jammu! Wow! I've always wanted to visit the Vaishnav Devi temple. I really am in Delhi and all of twenty-nine years, truth on both counts. How old are you?"

"Okay ma'am, I am Aakash Ahmed, thirty-two years old, and have a bookshop in Jammu. Bachelor still. Why? Because … hey, I never found the perfect woman, don't even know if she exists - don't claim to be a saint by any standards either, lol. So, are you going to tell me your real name? Because fiction I have plenty of in my library."

"Amrita, and I..." She hesitated wondering how much she ought to reveal, sighed and typed on, "I am just a plain old housewife and mom to two adorable eight year old twin girls."

"Just? You use the words 'just' when you talk about yourself. There's more to you Amrita than meets the eye. Talk to me; tell me what's eating you? What a nice girl like you is doing in the wicked world of cyber chat. I want to know the Amrita who's not just a 'just'. You don't know me nor I you. This might 'just' be what the doctor ordered."

Little did Aakash know how true his words would ring. For the first time on the net, after ages in her real life too, Amrita could actually be herself. Laugh and cry and talk about things that were bottled inside her for so long that even she was unaware of the many ways in which they had affected her personality. Amrita was not Mrs. Rahul Sud when she was chatting with Aakash; she was Amrita - the person. The self she knew a lifetime ago. It was both fantastic and intimidating at the same time. Treading a path that seemed safe enough, for this was the virtual world, wasn't it? Yet in her heart she knew she was betraying Rahul. On the other hand, what was he doing to her? She was justified, she told herself, this was important for her to maintain her sanity; this was the therapy that would keep her afloat. Longing to be with Aakash and waiting like a schoolgirl for the appointed hour of the meet, she found herself slowly but surely getting physically and mentally attracted to him.

Aakash too fell in love with her, a woman whom he had met but perchance on the net. She would be a relationship like the many he had already had, he had thought. Amrita's sensitivity, intelligence, wit and sexuality had come across the miles and onto his computer screen. She was the kind of woman he thought existed only in fantasy - a complete woman! More importantly, she made him feel whole again. What cruel game was fate playing with him? After all these years a woman actually warmed the cockles of his heart and not only was she a virtual friend but she belonged to someone else. She was a married woman.

CHAPTER 2

Casual conversations gave way to personal ones and lighthearted flirting turned into full-blown attraction. It began with exchanging hugs during their interludes, hugs that felt very warm and real. Then during one of their intense conversations Aakash kissed her with a simple word on her screen. This was definitely crossing the barrier she thought; this was an affair! Be it a virtual or a real one, it amounted to the same deceit. Despite her sensibilities she found herself slipping into the quicksand of her emotions.

"Aakash."

"Jaan."

"Jaan? Am I that?" she enquired incredulously.

"You are that. My life blood - my Jaan."

"And how many girls have been honoured with this endearment?"

"I don't know about others, I have but one heartbeat running through me and it is called Amrita."

"Oh, Aakash." She sighed as she typed on, "I don't know what to say."

"Amrita, we have to meet. Please, please come to Jammu." Aakash replied.

"What?" she could not believe her eyes.

"I would come to meet you, but it is far too dangerous to meet in Delhi. I've been thinking about it, the Vaishnav Devi visit that you always wanted to make would be your perfect alibi."

"Aakash!" Amrita's heart skipped a beat. She couldn't believe her ears. He was asking her to take this relationship from the virtual, where she could still control it, even delete and deny it, into the real. Legitimize it. Validate it. Make it one of the truths of her life.

"Listen Jaan, listen to me; listen to your heart. It is what we both want, what we both need and deserve." Aakash was pleading with her now. "We are mature adults and stealing some precious moments from our compromised lives won't harm anyone, in fact it will make us more complete and perhaps even the better for it. Do it, Jaan, just come here. I will accompany you to the temple and then bring you to your hotel. That one whole day that we get together will witness the union of two lost souls. Don't be scared, I will not do anything you wouldn't want me to. Just being with you in person, talking to you while looking at the real you, that's good for me for starters, lol," Aakash wrote.

She could sense that he wanted her to believe his sincerity even though he was trying to ease the gravity of his words.

"Aakash, stop." She found herself buckling in.

"Okay, okay, I'm sorry! But what say, can you make my dream come true?"

She thought about it, thought about the girls, her husband and their home. It was fine that Rahul was openly having an affair, but should he find out about this, what wrath would he bestow on her? Would he separate a mother from her children? Would he understand? Would he give a damn? What the hell, would he ever come to know? Aakash was right, they would never be able to meet in Delhi, and if she were going to give herself this chance, she would have to go to him. The temple visit was the perfect excuse. She had mentioned it before and he would never give it a second thought. Amrita had made enough sacrifices and deserved this break. It was now or never. She decided to take her chance.

"You've got it Aakash, your dream will come true. Rahul is on an overseas tour next Monday. I'll settle the girls in with my parents and fly down on Tuesday. Come and fetch me at the airport." Amrita's hands were trembling as she typed the words out.

Aakash had to pinch himself to believe what he was reading. Tuesday, and today was Thursday, only five days before he would hold in the palm of his hands the face of the woman who had captivated him so.

"Jaan," he typed, but Amrita could make out that it was barely a whisper and instantly felt the intensity with which he said it.

"Nothing more Aakash, don't say anything more. Let us just relish the anticipation. And don't keep me waiting, ok?" Amrita smiled as she wrote.

He was smiling too. "Sweet dreams, my love, and don't worry I'll be there long before your flight lands. Thank you my angel. I love you."

CHAPTER 3

Sweet dreams indeed! It was a miracle that she managed to keep a straight face through the next five days for her heart was going crazy. Rahul's departure on Monday brought with it a sense of relief and freedom. He had shown initial surprise when Amrita announced her programme and had also suggested she take her mother or a friend along. Amrita had managed to convince him that she wanted to be by herself and do this alone. It was fine by him if that was what she wanted, he had told her. Then he had held her in his arms almost as though he was trying to tell her something, she felt. Guilty, but clear in her mind that this trip was a must for her self-respect, she kissed the girls, her parents and Mrs. Amrita Sud goodbye as the car sped to the airport the next morning.

Aakash could still not believe his good fortune. He was at the airport one hour before the scheduled arrival simply because the excitement had made him restless. It was as though he was already connected to her by just being there.

'Announcing the arrival of 9W 605 from New Delhi.' The microphone cackled.

His blood vessels were going to burst he felt, for his heart was beating so loud. Then the strangest thing happened - it was as though every one was walking in slow motion - faces after faces, but not the one he was looking for. He had formed an image of her in his mind and was sure he'd be able to spot her in the mêlée. She had never sent him her photograph nor had she revealed her last name. At the same time here was a girl who was ready to break many a norm and put much at stake just for him.

Then it happened; she emerged on the escalator. His fantasy had come alive. She was gliding through, pushing her shoulder length hair away from her face, adjusting the handbag over her shoulder, her eyes scanning the arrival lounge for the face she had only seen on her computer screen.

Aakash hid behind the crowd without taking his eyes off her for a second. She looked so ethereal in her exquisitely cut, plain off-white suit. Fair and clear complexioned, she carried herself with an air of dignity. He wanted to savour this moment.

Amrita stepped off the escalator and slowly made her way toward the exit lounge. For a moment she thought Aakash wasn't there for she couldn't see him in the throng of waving arms. She walked up even more slowly now with a hint of worry on her brow. Had she made a fool of herself? Was this a sick joke that was played on her? She wanted to turn around and run back. Just as the seeds of doubt were about to germinate into full-blown dejection her face lit up and she stopped dead in her tracks. For, with an impish smile that reached his eyes, Aakash stepped into her line of vision. Tall, tanned, fit and ruggedly good looking with thick black hair carelessly pushed back, dressed casually in blue jeans and a white shirt, he looked quite the unassuming debonair that he wasn't.

Time stood still for the two of them. Amrita walked up toward the exit and straight to where Aakash was waiting for her. Her face was flushed and her eyes bright with excitement. Aakash wanted to take her in his arms that instant and hold her possessively, but they were at the airport and he didn't want to rush things for her.

She looked up and saw him smiling, his gaze transfixed on her, content only to see and in no hurry to speak.

She broke the silence, “Aakash?”

“Jaan, you’re beautiful,” he said softly. Then to break the awkwardness of the moment he added, “Did you have a pleasant flight?”

“Yes, thank you,” she managed, “You scared me, you know. I thought you hadn’t come.”

He winked at her, “I know and I enjoyed that.”

“Horrible man.”

“That’s me. Let’s go love.” He took her overnighter and guided her towards his car. He held the door for her as she got into the passenger seat in front, and then after placing her bag on the rear seat he sat behind the wheel, looked at her and smiled, “ So this is my precious Amrita.” She nodded, too tongue-tied to say anything, unable to believe herself that she was actually with him.

“You are gorgeous, did you know that?” He saw her cheeks change colour. “How lucky can a man get? I want to thank you Amrita for making this trip.”

CHAPTER 4

Amrita was at peace with herself. There were no need for words; many a word had been exchanged over the last few months. They knew each other better than they knew themselves. It seemed the most natural thing in the world for them to be driving off together. Like it was meant to be so. It was time now to just enjoy being in each other's company and let the strains of Claderman's piano, playing on the radio, complement this magical moment.

"How are the kids?" Aakash asked her.

"Very well," Amrita said. Then turning in her seat she faced him. "May I make a request?"

"Sure."

"I know you mean well Aakash, but please don't mention the kids, my home or my life in Delhi. I want to be me. Free of responsibilities, free of guilt, free to be a hundred percent with you. Am I making sense?" she bit her lips and looked at him just a little bit embarrassed.

"Yes Ma'am, all the sense in the world. I can understand that. From this moment on it is going to be only you and me. Right?" Aakash replied with a scout's salute and Amrita could now see for herself how his lips curled with his indulgent smile.

Without thinking she gently jabbed her fist into his arm. "Right," she said. His arm felt strong and muscular to her. It was the first physical contact they had ever had and was enough to send sweet sensations through both their bodies.

He grimaced in mock hurt "Ouch! Lady Hitler, are you?" he said while rubbing his supposedly injured arm.

Reveling in each other's company they were in high spirits by the time they arrived at the hotel when the music playing on the radio was abruptly interrupted.

"This is All India Radio. We are interrupting this programme for a special news flash. An assassination was attempted on the Prime Minister of India. At 12:30pm IST, the Prime Minister, Mr. Inder Sahni, was returning to his residence when five Jihads from Pakistan Occupied Kashmir ran towards his cavalcade and blew themselves up by throwing themselves onto the car. The special bulletproof car took most of the impact, but turned turtle with the magnitude of the force. The PM was rushed to The All India Institute of Medical Sciences in a very critical condition. He has sustained spinal and cerebral injuries. A deep fracture in his skull is the immediate area of concern. Teams of specialists are in attendance. A statement released by Dr. U.N. Krishnan, the chief neurologist, states that the PM is still unconscious. Effort is being made to keep the heamatoma controlled, but his condition is very unstable.

The Deputy Prime Minister, Mr. Ranjeet Roy, has taken charge and will be addressing the nation at 6:00pm IST. All border areas in Jammu and Kashmir have been told to evacuate and have been put on Red Alert. Hindu-Muslim tension is already evident in New Delhi and is expected to build up in other states too. The deputy PM and the Indian Army have appealed to the citizens of India to help them maintain law and order. Mr. Roy has declared a state of emergency in the country with an indefinite curfew in the capital. A special news bulletin will be broadcast every half hour. This is the end of this special bulletin. "

They sat numb in the car. Aakash turned the car around and drove out of the hotel, he was thinking much ahead and there was no way he was going to leave Amrita alone now, not even for a moment.

"What are you doing?" Amrita wanted to know. Aakash worked the winding road at a dangerous speed.

"Talk to me Aakash, you're scaring me, where are we going?"

"You heard of the Hindu-Muslim riots breaking out in the country. Have you ever witnessed one Amrita?" His face was grim and his body tense. He looked straight ahead at the road. "I have, first hand. I was eight years old then. Haven't you ever wondered why I have a Hindu first name and a Muslim surname? Aakash Ahmed, son of Radha and Aftaab Ahmed. They were college sweethearts who believed in the secular India that Gandhi envisioned. Happily married with a daughter and a son, they settled in the scenic valley of Srinagar. They were a close knit, content family."

He looked at her, Amrita was all ears, "Go on Aakash," she coaxed him on. He was talking in the past tense and she knew in the pit of her stomach that what was coming next would be as difficult for Aakash to say as it would be for her to hear.

"When the Hindu-Muslim riots broke out in Kashmir during the '71 war there was murder in the eyes of both communities. Each claimed their right over the territory and the result was unbridled rage. My family was a victim of that carnage. I lost my parents and older sister in that inhuman lust for power. I escaped because I was small enough to hide inside a suitcase." He sighed. "I have been there, Jaan and I know how unsafe it is for you to stay in that hotel now. The hotel staff can themselves turn on you. Hate in the name of religion is a deadly weapon. I am taking you to my farmhouse on the outskirts of Jammu; you will be safe there. When things cool down you can return home to Delhi." He looked at her, "Trust me?"

"Of course I trust you, I wouldn't be here otherwise." She smiled and then added, "I am sorry to hear about your parents and sister. Is that one of the reasons why you didn't marry?"

He laughed despite himself at her innocent observation and then replied on a more reflective note, "Marriage!" He exclaimed taken by surprise, then paused for a moment to sort his thoughts and continued, "Most people marry for all the wrong reasons. Yes, memories of that tragedy will haunt me forever. Hate is a very strong emotion, but I have not lost faith in the power of love. I have been around Jaan, but marriage? I reckon you're right. Maybe I have been looking for the kind of love that my parents shared. None of my girlfriends inspired me enough to even think about marriage. When I finally met someone special, she was already spoken for." He looked at her and smiled and Amrita realized with a jolt, that he was talking about her. "Marriage is the uniting of two souls in a bond that even they cannot break, not this ritualistic farce that most people live."

Amrita was reflecting on the profundity of his words while absorbing the breathtaking view of this mountainous winter capital of Kashmir. She thought about her shallow marriage and of all the reasons that had made her commit to it and stay committed. The news flash came to mind once again. She wasn't worried about the twins; they would be safe with her parents. They must be concerned about her though, she thought. The car came to a halt and brought her back to the present. Aakash switched off the engine and looked at her apologetically.

"Hey, why so quiet? I touched a raw nerve didn't I? Sorry. I didn't mean to …"

"Love is ..." she put a finger on his lip. "Haven't you read *Love Story*?"

He kissed her finger before replying, "'... never having to say you're sorry.'"

Embarrassed, but enjoying the intimacy, she brought her hand back to her lap and clasped them together.

He said nothing for a while; only beamed at her. Then said very softly, "So there is love."

It was her turn to look at him and let her smile and her eyes allow him a guess.

Laughing, he got out and then opened the door for her, "There is a phone booth in this store. Would you like to tell your folks that you are safe and will make your way back as soon as it is possible?"

Did he read her mind? Amrita was touched by his thoughtfulness. She did as she was told and spoke to her parents and children, reassuring them that she was safe and with an old schoolmate. Rahul, she was told, had cancelled all his meetings and was trying to come back to Delhi as soon as the curfew was lifted. He was worried and concerned about her, her father had said.

CHAPTER 5

Amrita felt uneasy after that phone call. Rahul was worried and concerned about her? That's a new one, she thought. It was probably just her father's inaccurate interpretation of the conversation.

Her hand was on the seat beside her and her fingers were fidgeting with the strap of her handbag. Aakash saw this and gently placed his hand on hers while continuing to drive with the other.

"Don't worry, Jaan, there's nothing we can do but wait. In a few days the heat will die down and all will be well with the world once again. Relax and enjoy the bonus vacation we've got."

The tension had eased as they were now climbing a remote hill that was seldom frequented even by the locals. Aakash knew for a fact that they would be very safe over there. Amrita felt a warm wave go through her body at the touch of Aakash's hand. She moved her thumb slightly so that she could wrap it around his fingers. Her cheeks were red, eyes moist and her lips wore a coy smile. Aakash wanted to take her there and then in the car itself, but he knew better than that.

They drove in silence for a while with Aakash holding her hand as he drove. She felt loved and desired. Finally able to relax and not be selfconscious in Aakash's company, she was able to absorb the natural scenic beauty around her once again.

"Just look at the mountains, aren't they beautiful?"

She exclaimed, still mesmerized by them. "I'm in love with them," she said turning to him.

"They are female, you can't do that - it's disgusting." He feigned horror.

She broke into laughter. "Female! What makes you so sure they are female?"

"They are treacherous too, are they not? Stonehearted and all." He smiled at his own wit and then added, " If they decide to turn on you, you wouldn't stand a chance. Disturb them and they get all upset and spill over. When a woman gets really angry haven't you heard of the phrase 'It's like a volcano erupting'?"

"Stop it. Not true." She was hysterical with laughter and unable to defend the integrity of her species she pretended to beat him up with both hands.

"See? I told you, when they don't know what else to do they crack up too."

The sound of their laughter lay like a warm blanket on the road they travelled.

"Look at it this way," she suggested looking at the magnificent ranges once again, "Mountains rise so majestically from the plains, nurture life and inspire love, to finally leave all these behind in their solitary journey upward bound, reaching out it seems with the tip of their fingers, in their quest to merge with their God - the sky."

"Oh my God girl! You have the heart of a poet. A philosophical poet!" he observed.

She wasn't done. Still enraptured by the enigmatic peaks she continued where she had left off. "Dressed in a veil of white purity it has nothing to offer but its true self. The sky in turn reaches out and keeps it constantly bathed in its cloud of love."

"Wow! I change that to romantic poet."

"My goodness, but this is almost as beautiful as the mountains. Aakash is this your farmhouse?" she exclaimed when the farmhouse came into view.

The farmhouse had been his dream. A wooden cottage equipped with all the modern amenities. Patios on every side of the cottage that over looked vast open green fields and the pine forest beyond. The deck in the living room had been extended onto a riverbed so that in summer when the melting snow gave more spirit to the river, it would flow beneath it. He had sold the Srinagar property and made this haven in memory of his lost family. He came here every weekend and planned to one day retire and write novels over here from dawn to dusk.

He lifted a big rock near the doorstep and retrieved the keys as though performing and act of magic. "Voilà," he said and showed her in.

The door opened into a big living room and an open kitchen that looked modern and well equipped. Amrita helped to bring in the fresh groceries and packed food that Aakash had picked up at the store, while Aakash took her bag to the bedroom on the first floor. He returned to the kitchen to find the kettle whistling on the stove and Amrita busily opening and shutting the cabinets till she had found the cups, tea, sugar and milk. She turned around and found him leaning against the door with his hands in his pockets, smiling indulgently at her. She smiled back, "Tea? I'm starved, you know how uninteresting the airline food is and then to top it off all this driving and tension didn't help either."

"You look like you've always been here, so at home." He said to her as she poured him a cup. He brought out the marble cake and cookies, and opened the box of sandwiches that they had just picked up.

"Hope the tea's okay, I haven't cooked in ages." She

apologized.

"Even if you had put salt in it instead of sugar, for me this cup of tea would have tasted divine."

He was looking into her eyes as he took his first sip, "Hey, did you actually put salt in it?" He grimaced.

"Wha..." and then she saw that he was laughing at her. "You wicked, ungrateful man," she said throwing the napkin at him.

"Boy! You do get violent, I'd better be careful around you." He said, catching the napkin before it found its mark, still laughing at her reaction.

They enjoyed the tea and a good tuck-in.

"Come on, let's go for a walk." He suggested, "It's beautiful outdoors at this time of the day."

She started clearing up.

"Forget the dishes, just grab your jacket."

The afternoon sun made a valiant effort to make its presence felt, but was no match against the cold wind. Amrita tucked both her hands deep into her jacket pockets to keep them warm. Aakash shut the door behind them and then as if it was the most natural thing in the world, he put one hand in his pocket and the other around her shoulders. They strolled along the river and stopped every now and again to drink it's crystal clear water or to throw pebbles into it and see them splash in and disappear. Aakash was having a grand time just watching her. Being well aware of the compromised life she led, he revelled in seeing her able to unleash and rejoice her free spirit. Her happiness was contagious and he too shed his mantle of inhibition and happily joined her in all her antics. She was behaving like an excited teenager and she couldn't care less. With Aakash, at least, she wanted to be herself. No pretences and no facades. They jumped over large rocks, crossed the river and made their way across the greener slopes towards his orchard. Aakash pointed out the mountain birds, the special flowers and told her folk stories related to local superstition. Every now and again he would smile at her and his eyes would stop at her lips.

When they arrived at the apple orchard Amrita could not believe her eyes. There were scores of trees resplendent with the red fruit. Amrita was wide eyed with excitement.

"Go ahead Eve, do your number on the forbidden fruit." He teased.

"You're asking for trouble Adam, who am I to deprive you." She quipped back and tried to jump and break off a bright red apple higher up on a tree. Aakash saw her delight and loved the childish giggle at each failed attempt.

"Come here you silly girl." He turned her around to him and lifted her.

"Oh my God!" she exclaimed, but the joy in her eyes and her smile was complete. She stretched up and plucked two ripe apples and then looked down at him her face aglow with exhilaration. He was still holding her up. She put her hands on his shoulders for support and ever so slowly he brought her down. She was pressed close to him and his strong arms held her firmly there. She could hear his heart beating in his chest and was sure he could hear hers. While his left hand held her firmly in place his right hand slid down her back and came to rest on the lower part of her spine. He pulled her even closer to him till she felt the urgency of his desire and the ache within herself too. She looked up at him and saw both, love and passion, in his eyes. She knew he was restraining himself, waiting for her consent. She put her palms to his cheeks and he turned his face to kiss it. She brought her hand down to his neck and then traced the outline of his lips with her fingers.

"Oh God! Jaan, please, you're driving me crazy."

Aakash whispered into her hair as one hand tightened around her and the other caressed her lower back into submission. Amrita succumbed to her passion, pressed herself into him and buried her face in his neck.

"Aakash, I've never felt this way before, tell me I'm doing the right thing."

He just held her close to him till they were both more in control of themselves. She needed more time he realized; he didn't want to seduce her. He wanted her to want him as dearly as he wanted her. It had to be a mutual need, a physical union that was pure, with no trace of deceit, sin or guilt.

"Let's go back to the cottage, it's getting dark and soon you'll have to deal with more wolves besides the one standing in front of you." He kissed her on the nose and led her back.

She understood his hesitation and was grateful for it. "Race you back, big boy." And off she went giving herself a good head start.

"Hey cheater, wait for me." He called out and gave chase.

CHAPTER 6

Once in the cottage, Aakash showed Amrita to her room. "Make yourself comfortable Jaan and if there's anything you need just give me a holler. Come down when you're rested, I'll be waiting impatiently." He kissed her on the forehead and then left the room closing the door behind him.

Amrita felt light-hearted and happy. The place itself was so beautiful, and to be here with Aakash - her heaven was complete. She unpacked the few clothes she'd brought along for the trip into the wooden almirah and then took a shower. The hot water eased away all remnants of stress from her body. The aroma of the eucalyptus trees, the purity of the air and the natural earthiness of the place, combined with all the love and attention she was getting, went a long way in liberating her. All the walls that she had built around her over the years were washed away. How much joy there was in simplicity, she thought. This was all she had asked for out of life, to love and to be loved.

She emerged from her room with her hair still damp, wearing a warm tracksuit and socks, a mixed aroma of shampoo and moisturizer emanating from her. Dancing flames from the fireplace lit the living room. A bottle of wine, glasses and a platter of cheese were placed on the coffee table. The room looked cozy and she basked in its warmth. Aakash had showered too and changed into jeans and a sweatshirt. Through the French window she could see him loading the barbecue. She opened the door and shivered as the cold breeze went through her hair.

Aakash's heart skipped a beat when he looked up and saw her standing beside him. Oblivious of the effect she was having on him she bent down to breathe in the aroma of the food. "Hmm delicious," she said.

"Yes," he whispered with a naughty smile as he took in her fragrance. She stood up and this time it wasn't the chill that made her shiver. Aakash ran his fingers through her hair, then curled them around the back of her neck and drew her to him. "Absolutely delicious!" He said looking straight into her upturned face.

The moon shone bright in the clear star-studded night. The only sounds that could be heard were that of the river flowing under them and of the barbecue spluttering. It seemed as though they were the only two people in the world.

"Amrita, I love you so much and it hurts to know that you belong to someone else," he said.

She put her hands very tentatively on his chest and took a step to close the physical distance between them, "Aakash, I am here now and I am yours."

He lowered his head and kissed her on the lips, a gentle but passionate kiss. He could feel himself getting aroused but had to look into her eyes to see her reaction. He smiled because her eyes were closed but her parted lips had a language of their own. When she opened her eyes he was relieved and amply satisfied with what he saw in them. She saw him smiling at her and wrapped her arms around his neck and smiled back in mutual acknowledgment. This time when they kissed it was with all the astral bodies witness to the unison of the two souls.

He took her inside the cottage, sat her on the couch in front of the fireplace and poured out the wine for both of them.

"To us Jaan," he toasted.

"To us," she replied and they both emptied their glasses, laughing at the end of it.

They drank wine, nibbled at the Swiss cheese and relished the barbecued trout that the workmen at the orchard had gifted them, recapitulating previous conversations on the net and soaking the warmth of the fire. All these had a heady effect on them both. Inhibitions overcome, they were now in a euphoric world of their own.

"More wine Jaanu?" Aakash asked her.

"You've got to be kidding, my love, I'm higher than a kite already."

She replied, holding the glass up for more. He laughed along with her. "You know what I'd love is some of that chocolate you keep on the kitchen table." She spoke softly as she rested her back against his chest. They were both on the carpet now, sitting with their legs stretched out in front of them, absolutely at peace with themselves and the world.

"Get the chocolate and leave my vantage place? Never." He said holding her close. "On second thought, let me get it for my princess and then make her pay the price for it." He had a wicked gleam in his eyes as he made her comfortable against some cushions and went off.

'If this is a dream - please don't wake me up,' she prayed.

"Here we go," he said sitting close to her again and showing her the bar of chocolate. "Oh no, not so fast, my precious, you want it, you come and get it." With that he broke a piece off the bar and held it between his teeth.

Amrita looked at him most amused. This was childish

but so romantic. She turned around in his arms to face him, then bit by bit she ate the chocolate till she had to pry the last bite from his teeth. Instead, she took his lower lip between hers and nibbled at it gently. She would look at him and repeat the whole thing teasing him with her mouth. When finally she went for the last bite his resilience broke and he gathered her in his arms.

"Jaan," he groaned as he pushed all but one cushion away and lay her down on the carpet. "I can't hold myself any longer," he whispered as he lay on top pushing himself into her, his hands exploring the wonderful swell of her breasts. She had been waiting for this moment and moaned in ecstasy when she felt his hands slip under her clothes and explore her entire body. He undressed himself and then her and by the light of the fire they made love for a long, long time.

Time had lost all meaning; it was only the dying fire and the ensuing chill that brought them out of their magical union.

Aakash raised himself on one elbow and stroked her hair, "You look so beautiful," he said to her. Amrita was flushed and had a very content radiance about her; the fire of passion still burning strong in her eyes each time Aakash kissed her. He stood up and pulled her up gently; lifting her in his arms he carried her up to her room.

"Bath or bed?" he asked her.

"Both," she replied sleepily.

"I'll be back with some hot cocoa," he said putting her down. "Love you."

"Me too," she replied.

By the time he came back dressed in his pajamas and a Pashmina dressing gown, Amrita was already in bed, busy writing into a diary. She gladly accepted the hot drink and sipped her way slowly through it while Aakash adjusted the logs to temper the fire.

"This should keep you comfortable enough." He looked at her from the fireplace. Freshly bathed and all cuddled up she made quite a tempting picture. "What is that?" he asked.

"Just a diary I write sometimes. A piece of my heart, you could say. I'll show it to you someday."

"I have you, I need nothing more," he said to her with all the love in the world in his eyes.

She blushed and changed the topic, "The cocoa was very good."

She thanked him as he took the empty mug from her. How could he be so sensitive and yet be so much of a man, she thought. How lucky she felt to be such a special person in his life.

"Goodnight, sweet one, and dream of me." Aakash kissed her on her nose and shut the door behind him.

Amrita had every reason to fall asleep immediately; the rhythmic sound of the river, the effect of the wine, their lovemaking, the warm bath and the hot cocoa, but she lay wide awake. Kaleidoscopes of images were making her restless. She tossed and turned but nothing worked and she knew why. She got out of bed and went straight for her bedroom door. The living room was almost dark but for the glowing embers. She knocked on Aakash's door and he opened it almost instantly.

"I can't sleep," she said, "I'm scared."

He let her step inside and then took her in his arms. "It's okay, come and sleep with me, I'll protect you from the boogie man." He tried a light quip, but there was concern in his voice.

She gladly got into bed with him. He was almost laughing when he said, "If you wanted to sleep with me you should have just said so, its what I wanted too. You didn't have to bring the boogie man into it, you know."

"Stop it, I was really scared, okay?" She chided him as she snuggled into the circle of his arm, her fingers drawing designs on his chest.

"Really? And what was scaring my precious?" He asked, relishing the fact that she was actually sharing his bed with him.

"Too many mixed up thoughts about my family, this assassination, and thoughts about your family too. I couldn't bear the thought of that child coming out of hiding only to find his loved ones in a pool of blood. It scared me Aakash." She confessed.

He held her close to him. Images of that gruesome day flashed before his eyes ever so often. He had learnt to deal with the pain but was touched that Amrita could empathize with him so. Now it was his turn to comfort her.

"Do you know why my parents named me Aakash?" He was caressing her arm as he reflected and didn't wait for a reply, "Because the sky belongs to everyone and no one can divide it. It has an eternal quality and is above, much above, the unstable elements that constitute this world and its denizens. They had this idealistic dream that people would not consider each other different on racial and regional grounds. That post-independence we would all live peacefully, that the skies would be the limit for the power of love. Aakash was born off these sentiments. You know Jaan, the funny thing is that even I am that audacious, I have the same dream." He kissed her hair. The intimacy was healing deep wounds in both.

"I guess if we ever have a son, we could call him

Amber. Then if we have another son we could call him Gagan. And then, my angel, we will have to have daughters because I don't know any more synonyms for Aakash." With this he managed to lighten her mood for they were both laughing. They spoke about the day's events, their lovemaking, and then held each other as sleep finally won over words.

CHAPTER 7

The morning sun filtered through the crack in the curtains. Amrita opened her sleepy eyes and blinked several times as consciousness set in. She was in Aakash's bedroom. It was cozy enough and yet every bit a man's room in its décor. A large mahogany table holding his laptop and books predominated the room. There was a Kashmiri rosewood antique almirah against the wall opposite the bed. An exquisite carpet lay between the bed and the writing table, facing the fireplace adding warmth to the room. The fireplace had a wooden mantle that held some more books supported by wrought iron horse head bookends. In the centre was a large wrought iron photo frame bearing Aakash's family photograph. He's taken after his father Amrita thought and has his mother's dark hair. She turned to look at him but he was not in bed. Taking in his fragrance from the pillow next to hers she got out of bed and went looking for him. The French windows were open and Aakash was cleaning out the barbecue.

"Good morning Sunshine, and did my angel sleep well?" he wished her.

"Morning," she kissed him. "Yes, I did, thank you. Let me help you."

"Then make me some tea like you did yesterday." He requested.

"Certainly, and what would you like for breakfast?" She asked him perfectly innocently.

His eyes turned passionate and his lips curled into his

characteristic smile. She blushed as she read the message in his eyes, surprised at her need for him too first thing in the morning.

"Allow me ma'am, I'll fix you a gourmet breakfast." He was laughing.

They worked in harmony, teasing each other as they went about their chores. Breakfast was a hearty affair and they had it on the deck watching the river dance and the birds sing. The dream was complete.

"We'll go down to the marketplace to catch up on the news. We do not get any radio waves up here." Aakash suggested once they were done and the dishes stashed away, "Want me to come with you into your shower just in case the boogie man turns up?"

"Good try, sweets, but I'll handle him myself if you don't mind." She'd caught on to him and teased him back.

"Oh really? Okay, I'll be in my room just in case. Come running to me. Naked preferably," He said half in jest, half lustfully.

She was wearing blue jeans with a pink shirt and white sneakers and had borrowed Aakash's dark blue pullover that she had tied around her waist.

"Going to college, sweetheart?" He winked holding open the car door for her. "You look too young to be messing with a dirty old man."

"And you are actually too young to be messing with a married woman," she replied.

"Hey, can I help it if she finds me drop dead gorgeous?" He proclaimed.

As they approached the market place and the radio waves came within reach, their car radio cackled to life. Aakash turned down the engine and tuned into the news. They had to wait a few minutes for the next news bulletin.

"This is a special news broadcast from All India Radio. An assassination had been attempted yesterday on the incumbent Indian Prime Minister, Mr. Inder Sahni, as he was returning to his office from Parliament. Twenty-four hours after the attempted assassination, he still remains comatose and is in a critical condition. Life-sustaining machines continue to keep his vitals signs stable. The doctors refrain from commenting on his prognosis at this stage. The country remains in a state of shock. Multi-religious meets are praying for the Prime Minister's speedy recovery and emphasizing the need for peace and unity in this hour of test. Although security has been beefed up, sporadic violence has been reported in the valley of Srinagar with the situation tense all over the state of Jammu and Kashmir. Curfew over New Delhi has been lifted, but the entire country remains in a state of emergency. The acting Prime Minister has said, in no uncertain terms, that India will not tolerate terrorism and will declare war against Pakistan if necessary, to ensure the safety of its citizens and the dignity of the country. The …"

Aakash tuned into the local channel and was listening very intently. Even though Amrita could not understand the language, she knew the news wasn't good. Aakash switched off the radio and sat back in his seat.

Very seriously he said to her, "Radio Pakistan is spreading propaganda against India. It has asked all Muslims worth their salt to stand up and fight for a free Kashmir. They want to make Kashmir a purely Muslim and independent country. You know what this means Jaan? It means the birth of many more Aakashs's. It means blind hate of one's own brother. It means we can trust no one now. These marketfolks and my workmen know you are here with me, but are unaware of your identity. You don't wear the traditional dress of the Muslim women and so they will be suspicious. We have to act fast."

He turned on the ignition and spoke to her as he drove back to the cottage. "When were you scheduled to return?"

"Evening flight, today," Amrita said with mixed emotions, fear on one hand and the painful thought of leaving Aakash on the other.

"With the curfew lifted that flight will take off as scheduled. If we leave now we'll make it in good time," he said turning into the driveway of the cottage. "Pack up as quickly as you can and come down."

Silently, with tears in her eyes, Amrita went to her room and mechanically put her clothes in the overnighter. She looked around her room, loving everything about it and wondering when she would come here again, if ever. If she could do it once she would do it again, she vowed to herself. She would be back one day, when the skies became the limit for the power of love, she thought.

Amrita came down the stairs very slowly, tears rolling unchecked down her cheeks. Aakash was leaning against the kitchen table looking down at and stroking a black garment. He looked up at her. In his eyes she saw for the first time a pain so deep that her heart went out to him. She dropped her bag and walked straight into his open arms. They held each other and cried and kissed and kept holding each other as if life itself depended on it.

"Come on Jaanu, we have to get you to the airport on time." He collected her overnighter and guided her to the door. He stopped to lock the cottage and then went to get the car. Amrita had walked ahead up the driveway and now stood looking at the distant trees. Aakash drove up and stretched across to open the door for her. She got in obediently.

He handed her the black garment. "This belonged to my mother Amrita. It was her favorite burkha. See the lace that makes the purda? My sister had made that for her. The design is a woman's prayer to the Lord seeking a long and prosperous life for her husband. Please wear it. Now. If we are stopped at any point, tell them your name is Muskan and that you are my 'begum'. Speak very softly and in Urdu."

She looked up at him and smiled, "I wish this journey takes forever and that every single person asks me this question."

He took her hand in his and drove towards the airport.

CHAPTER 8

You could cut the tension in the air with a knife. Amrita was grateful for Aakash's presence of mind, for they had escaped many an inquisition with her hiding behind the protective burkha.

"Amrita," She looked up in anticipation when he spoke at last. "The airport is only half an hour away from here and there's still over two hours for your flight. We've made it so far and I don't anticipate any trouble now. Soon you will board that plane and go back to your life." He took her hand in his again. "Although it was so short a time, barely a day, I have experienced enough happiness and love," he paused, "to last me a lifetime if necessary."

He kissed her hand and held it against his heart. "Promise me you won't let your husband walk all over you. You are a very special woman and it's high time he treated you like one. I don't mean to tell you how to live your life. You are an exceptionally intelligent, sensitive and mature person. I respect your decisions. I just want you to remember that although Aakash may be physically distanced from you he will always be yours. You are not alone so don't ever feel so. We may never meet again; I may become just a dream. So be it. But you only have to close your eyes and the dream will be yours again. Look to the skies and know that Aakash holds you in his love. It doesn't have to be so, but if you ever want this dream to come true, your Aakash but waits."

Amrita was crying, "Aakash where were you all my life? Why did you wait so long to come to me? I have never loved a man like I love you. I don't want to go back, please don't make me go, please." She was sobbing and pleading with him.

He pulled the car off the road and into a thick jungle and switched off the ignition. There was time enough for the flight, and he dare not stop on the road. Amrita crying helplessly was too much for him to bear.

"Come here Jaan," he pulled her to him, cradled her head on his chest, stroked her hair and let her vent her feelings.

"I don't want to go back, Aakash, " she cried into his chest, "I know I have to, but I don't want to. I don't want to leave you. Help me please Aakash, help me, please." She was clinging on to his shirt as though it was her lifeline.

He rocked her gently and stroked her hair till she calmed down, whispering to her, "It's okay, it's okay. You'll be all right. Look at me," he told her. She was reluctant to leave the comfort of his chest.

He put his finger under her chin and lifted her face. "Look at me Jaanu, and listen carefully to what I am saying. Who said this was going to be easy? On the contrary, we should be grateful to God for this precious gift that he has given to us. You aren't leaving me; you will always be with me in every breath that I take. My heart will beat to the rhythm of your name. I look forward to the day when you actually come back to me, but even then we will have to return to our lives because there are so many lives that depend on you."

Aakash's words consoled Amrita and she snuggled back to the comfort of his chest. "You are right," she said wiping her tears on his shirt and making him smile. "Those were very beautiful words you just spoke, you know. I want to add to it though to make it complete. You know the moon; it only shines bright because the sky darkens itself enough to allow it so. I am that moon and as long as I have my Aakash, I will always glow in his love."

They kissed passionately as if to seal their tryst with destiny.

"I guess I …" But before she could finish her thoughts the sounds of frenzied screams rang through the air, followed by gunfire and abusive shouting. They sat very quiet and very still. Aakash lowered the veil of the burkha over Amrita's face and without making any sound pulled out a revolver from the inner pocket of his jacket.

The car was well concealed by the thick forest, but an observant eye could spot it. Through the thicket they saw some masked men in long kurtas, brandishing their guns and bloody swords, laughing and chanting menacingly as they drove away in their jeep.

Aakash heaved a sigh of relief and said to Amrita, "Now you know why I want you out of here as fast as possible?"

She sat in stunned silence, paralyzed by this close encounter with death.

"Wait here, I'll be back in a minute." He said to her.

He opened the door as softly as he could and treaded very cautiously so as not to make any sound with his feet. He reached an opening from where he could view the road and yet not be visible himself. What he saw took him back to the time when he was a helpless eight-year-old. Pulled out of their horse carriage and murdered in cold blood were the mutilated bodies of a middle aged man and woman and three children, the youngest of them a boy, about seven to eight years old.

"Oh my God!" Aakash exclaimed under his breath and turned away.

He was visibly shaken when he came back to the car.

"What happened, Aakash?" She sensed his agitation.

He spoke very quickly. "Amrita, those men just killed an entire family, husband, wife and three children. It is a frightening sight. Those bastards were vicious."

He was thinking aloud, "The bodies are strewn all over the road and their cart has been destroyed. That makes it impossible to go ahead by road."

He looked at her, "The only other way to the airport is through the forest. We have to leave now, before another vehicle drives up. Come on, let's go."

She grabbed her purse and followed Aakash out of the car. He held her hand and guided her to the opening in the bush.

"Brace yourself, given half a chance I would have taken you through another route to protect you from this horrific sight, but this is the only way."

Amrita gasped at what she saw, her sobs stopped short in her throat and she wanted to be sick. But fear and Aakash's firm grip on her had her following him down to the road, quickly around the body of the little boy who lay in their path, and then further downhill through the forest towards the airport, as fast as their feet could take them. It was difficult. The forest had steep slopes and the ground was damp and slippery. Keeping in the cover of the protective trees was important too. Ever so often they would hear the maniacal chants of the fanatics and hide very still behind them. Out of breathe and completely exhausted they managed to reach the airport.

"Run Amrita, run. Go and check-in quickly."

She wanted to say something to him but he stopped her. "Check-in Jaan, please." He almost pushed her into the lounge.

The flight had been announced. Due to the emergency that had been imposed only passengers were allowed into the airport and once checked-in they had to remain in the security enclosure. Amrita made her way to the aircraft very slowly and with very mixed emotions. She didn't even have a chance to say goodbye to Aakash, to thank him for saving her life in more ways than one.

Aakash saw the flight take off, then he just slumped down and cried; tears of relief, anguish and frustration.

CHAPTER 9

As the flight attendant announced their landing in Delhi, Amrita's heart was yearning to go back to Aakash. She knew, of course, that her life was here. Someday she would meet him again, she was sure of that. As the reality of her life set in she realized that she still had the burkha on. In a swift movement she removed it and was surprised to find Aakash's blue pullover tied around her waist. She untied it and then hugged it. This was her omen; her Aakash was here with her.

Aakash took the local bus from the airport to his workplace in Jammu. He was anxious to hear from Amrita but the communication lines were yet another victim of the emergency. The next day Aakash went to retrieve his car. By some miracle it had gone unnoticed by even the authorities. He unlocked the door and sat inside. Amrita's overnighter was sitting proudly on the rear seat. He smiled as he touched the bag. It stood testimony of yesterday's dream as a part of today's reality.

The drive to the cottage brought back too many memories for him. Once there, Aakash delayed taking Amrita's bag to her room, not wanting to face the vacuum created by her absence. Instead, he sat on the deck drinking a cup of tea and stayed there letting the setting sun and cold wind numb the pain that had started deep within and then wrecked his entire being. When the moon shone in all its glory he walked to the edge of the deck, looked up at it, spread his hands out in a wide embrace and called out her name aloud for the entire universe to hear, "Amritaaaaa."

Fighting the void he finally made his way upstairs. He placed the bag on the table. Involuntarily his mind re-enacted the scenario of the previous evening. His eyes went to the bed where she lay cuddled so childlike. On it he saw a page torn out from her diary. He sat down to read it.

Dearest Aakash,

For as long as the river
flows, I will love you
But the river can dry up.
For as long as the trees grow
I will love you
But trees are destructible.
For as long as the birds sing,
I will love you
But birds too are mortal.
For as long as the flowers
bloom, I will love you
But even buds perish.
For as long as the sun
shines, I will love you
But the sun too gets eclipsed.
So I will love you for as long
as the skies exist,
I will love you for as long
Aakash.

Your Jaanu,
Amrita.

Aakash smiled and kissed her name with tears welling in his

eyes. He got up, went to the fireplace and built up a slow soothing fire to keep the room warm. Then he opened the almirah and unpacked her bag.

CHAPTER 10

1½ YEAR LATER

Amrita stood staring at the dimly lit garden. A thick blanket of fog had settled over it and once again she couldn't help but compare it to her own life.

Too much water had flowed under the bridge and she was completely lost at this point. Every ounce of her will power had gone into restraining herself from making contact with Aakash in the past few months, but now he seemed her only hope and she was scared and lost and needed to talk to him desperately.

She logged on. Her mailbox was full of mail that he had been sending to her ever since her return. She had saved them all. Some letters expressed his concern for her, others were full of love and about how much he missed her. When she didn't respond to them he stopped writing. She opened his last letter to her and read it for the nth time. Mustering up courage she then clicked on the reply button. She wasn't sure how much she should tell him but she had to make a start and contact him first. He was the only friend she had besides being the love she nurtured discretely and she missed him dearly. But it was after all a virtual friendship that had been taken to a different plane. Not in the heat of the moment, no, but as the natural culmination of a beautiful relationship. He may have moved on, she thought, why should she presume his loyalty? Nevertheless, he had sent her several mails and that gave her hope that maybe, just maybe, he was still waiting for word from her. The mails had stopped a long time ago, she had cut him off opting to give herself fully to her family rather than complicate her life with a dual existence, something she was incapable of. She would have given anything to be able to be with him, anything but her girls. She had always kept their happiness above hers. The equation in her life had changed now and she could, without guilt, indulge the deep vacuum within her that kept yearning for him. Did he still miss her too? She had to find out.

> Dear Aakash,
>
> You must be surprised to hear from me after all this while. It has been a very long time I know and I'm sorry. Sorry for not replying to all your mails. Sorry for keeping you in suspense as to how I was. Sorry for putting you through the trauma of silence. I am deeply apologetic and hope you find it in your heart to understand and forgive me. What can I say but that 'Life' has been happening to me? That sounds funny I know but sometimes I feel God made a special script for the drama of my life. Anyway more about me once I hear from you.
>
> How have you been? The library and the writer's hideout, how are they doing?
>
> I know that I have no right to ask this of you but please do write to me, I long to hear from you.
>
> With Love,
> Amrita.
>
> P.S. I almost forgot to tell you, I've have been blessed with one more child, a very beautiful girl.

She sent the mail and sat back in her chair feeling the tension in her easing a little. She'd finally done something she had wanted to do a long time ago but circumstances then had held her back. She waited by the machine, feeling that the mere act brought her closer to Aakash. The baby moved in her crib and fell asleep again. The bonding was complete.

It had been a tumultuous homecoming for her from the eventful trip to Jammu. All had been delighted that she had returned home safe. Rahul too had cut his trip short and when he arrived the next morning the family it seemed had come together in a very real sense. Something about him was different; she had sensed that even before she'd left for Jammu. Now he was the indulgent husband and doting father that he had been many years back. The Rahul whom she had lost to money and power and Gayatri seemed to be back. She didn't question him; she'd learnt to accept his moods a long time back. She had never seen her girls so happy, nor had she seen him enjoy their company so much. It was as though he had suddenly rediscovered his family. She wasn't sure what this was all about or how long it would last, but if any good came out of that terrible assassination attempt it was that the four of them were truly united.

What a time, she thought, for this to happen. She was deeply in love with Aakash and the thought of anyone else touching her intimately was loathsome. But force herself into reality she did and much as her body and heart screamed she completely disconnected from Aakash and merged into Mrs. Amrita Sud once again.

The pregnancy came as a complete shock. Rahul was delighted, for he longed for a son. Amrita was completely traumatized. She wasn't sure whose baby she was carrying. She prayed it was Rahul's for she'd hate to deceive him, but deep in her heart somewhere she wanted it to be her love child. This was a predicament that she in her wildest dreams never thought she would be in. It was a nightmare she had wanted to wake up from. Her choices were limited. Aborting the baby certainly wasn't one of them. A part of Aakash and his love may be growing in her and the mere thought had been enough to give her the courage she had needed to do the right thing.

Time and again the entire scene played before her eyes. How she had called Rahul into this very room. There was something she had to tell him she had said. She had begged him to hear her out to the end. She had started with her life, the way it had been before he married her. How happy she had been in their early years despite having to give up her career plans and adjust to a new lifestyle. How humiliated and hurt she felt when Rahul openly flirted with other women and had mistresses the world knew about. How lonely she had been. How she had found Aakash. She shuddered as she recalled the colour draining from his face. She had felt terrible too. Her own self-respect would not allow her to let him live a lie, she had told him. Even now she broke into a sweat as she relived the rest of the conversation.

"You pushed me into his arms Rahul, can't you see that?" she had said as he slowly walked towards her, his face contorted with rage.

"So that was your religious rendezvous? Your meeting with your God?" He made God sound like a dirty word. He was standing so close to her that she could physically feel his fury.

"I had gone for that, honestly." Then she had looked down as though pleading guilty, "And to meet him too."

He slapped her right across her face. "You whore!" he had screamed.

She had not seen it coming and the impact made her fall back against the table.

"Why now? Why are you telling me this now? Why not before I touched you? Why not then? My wife, a whore! Goddamit Amrita, there's no difference between you and that Gayatri." He had turned away from her.

"Rahul…"

"Don't you want to know what made me come back to you?" He had turned to face her again. "You were different. I saw how shallow and materialistic those women were. Even Gayatri. How their kids went astray because the mothers had no time for them. You were different; you were my wife, the mother of my children. You were perfect. How could you?" He had turned away from her again.

"Another man touched my wife and made love to her. She made love to him. Dear God!" He had covered his eyes with the palm of his hand in complete disgust and despair, "It's finished." He looked distraught. "What we had is over. But this is your punishment, you will continue to live as my wife, you will give birth to my son and then…." He stopped short.

"This baby you are carrying, it is mine, isn't it? Or are you going to give birth to a bastard?" He was so angry that his words had sounded like a slow hiss escaping between his clenched teeth.

Tears had been streaming down her face and she could not meet his eyes. Her silence spoke louder than words.

"Talk to me Amrita, is the baby…." He roared, but a new strength surged through Amrita when he called her baby a bastard.

"I don't know," she shouted. "Enough is enough. How dare you threaten me, Rahul? You lost your right to that the first time you cheated on me. No, this baby may not be yours and that is your punishment," she cried back.

What happened then was so quick. Rahul had lunged towards her with the table lamp and rammed her on her forehead with it. She had screamed as loud as she could, to attempt to get help, instinctively knowing it was a question of survival for her and the baby. Before she blacked out completely, through a hazy consciousness, she saw him clutching his chest and slumping onto the floor too.

She had regained consciousness in the hospital. An enormous bandage covered a deep and painful gash on the side of her head. Rahul had suffered a massive stroke. He had survived it but barely. His vitals were functioning but the brain had been completely damaged. There had been a police inquiry and all she had told them was that she had tripped while trying to get to Rahul and thus hurt herself. Any doubt that she might have had about her baby's parentage was put to rest at the time her baby, Aasma, was born. Aasma was Rhesus positive. Both Amrita and Rahul were Rhesus negative. She now knew for sure that the baby was Aakash's.

The irony of it Amrita thought was that each one got their just desserts. Rahul was now completely at her mercy and not even aware of it. For all the years of betrayal that he had made her suffer, Aasma now carried his name and there was nothing he could do about it. Her child got the family name but she felt so responsible for Rahul's condition that her entire energy was devoted to taking care of him despite round the clock nursing care. The business demanded her attention too and so did Aasma, who was now nine months old. The twins, almost ten years old, were the worse hit but there was just so much she could do. She would spend what little time she could to talk to them and take interest in their daily lives. Alia was open and would pour her heart out to her and even keep Aasma with her on the nights that she had to travel for work.

Rhea seemed to have clammed up. It was impossible to penetrate her thoughts. Her friends and her life were her private affair. Her grades in school academics and sports were excellent and she was the school captain. Her teachers were happy with her performance but did voice concern over her moods. Most importantly Rhea was most caring toward her father. Even though he lay almost comatose she would talk and read to him constantly. So Amrita kept her reservations to herself.

A beep from her computer brought her back from her thoughts. She had received a mail from Aakash.

> Dear Amrita,
>
> I can only thank God that you wrote. Yes, you should have done so earlier- I was worried. A myriad of thoughts would run through my head and your silence made the possibilities worse. Those were very difficult days for me. I had to make a concerted effort to get on with my life. All I could do was pray for you. After reading your mail I know they were answered. I am relieved to know you are well. Congratulations on the birth of your daughter, I know she must be as pretty as you.
>
> I am now in the USA. Jammu had become too communal and I was mentally and emotionally unhappy there. The library no longer exists. The 'hideout', as you put it, is locked up. I don't see myself going there in the near or distant future. My life is here in the US that is so much more liberal and open to options.
>
> I missed you too but now rest in the knowledge that you are well. Write in whenever you wish to and even if you don't, it's ok. I know you are where you belong – safe in your home, and that is enough for me. I wish you and your family every happiness.
>
> Love,
> Aakash.

Amrita sat stunned in her chair. She read the mail over and over again to make sure she understood what he was trying to tell her. He had started over, a fresh life in the USA. There were no plans of returning. Even if she did not write it was ok with him. He had missed her – in the past tense? Did he try to tell her that her place was with her family? What had she expected? That he would be waiting all his life for her, till whenever she deigned to include him in hers?

She almost laughed at her own stupidity to have expected anything else. She reached for her diary:

If a fresh start is what he wants that is exactly what he will get. No point in imposing my problems or myself on him. And to tell him about Aasma would mean to never give him a chance to live his dreams, to hold and pin him down with my life choices. So I will end this chapter right here. Never again will I send him another mail or respond to any from him, if he ever writes again. I hope he does. It is painful. A pain I will have to learn to live with.

When the skies are the limit for the power of love,
Thence we shall meet and till then my love,
Live well your dreams, I move out of your way,
If the skies survive – we'll meet some day.

As the years got on she became very proficient at managing the business. Rahul's condition remained the same though physically he had become very frail. The girls had grown up into very attractive women. The twins were ready to leave for college. They would both go to Virginia, she had decided, it was a well-reputed university and offered both Business Studies as well as Psychology Honours, so Rhea and Alia could be together. What was more was that the campus dormitories maintained strict discipline, a rare feature these days. Besides, Monica, her school friend lived there and had agreed to be their guardian. Rhea the headstrong and Alia the gullible, she was grateful Monica would be there to settle them in and keep an eye on them for her.

There was no way she could leave Rahul. The only times she did was when she was compelled to leave for work. He was terribly weak now and optimum care with hourly monitoring was prescribed. The doctors were surprised that he had survived this long and lauded Amrita for the care she took of him, but she knew in her heart that had it not been for her he may not have been compromised in the first place. Never for a moment did she feel any guilt or remorse. Aasma was her strength, a living proof of her womanhood and her love.

She poured her heart out to the only friend she had left, her diary.

I THINK OF YOU

The sun sets,
Darkness pervades,
Not a star lights the sky
as I sit by my window
thinking …

A thousand sounds
 infiltrate through the
 night.
But my ears hear only the
 sounds of incessant
 crying – devoid of tears.
Heart rending screams
– of zero wavelengths.
As my palms close over my ears,

My eyes drop their curtain shutting the world,
And I fight to take in oxygen to quench my aching lungs,
I think of you.

When lightning strikes shaking my world,
And the howling wind won't leave me alone,
When lonesome streets threaten to swallow me,
Lonely stretches of miles enhance my woes.
I gather myself – step into my dreams.
Search the entire landscape of my memory.
Faces appear…then fade
– like traffic lights.
Only a few helped me at the crossroads.
I think of you.

I think of you…
and a strange soothing envelopes me,
My soul gets uplifted; warmth spreads through me.
and my life seems to go back all those years
Relive all our happiness; relive all my tears.
and once again I feel it still is yesterday
When you and I sang our love song, unhappiness stood far away.

A strange turning did my life take
Into loneliness and fear.
Treading these unknown miles alone
Your gentle voice I long to hear.

Maybe…one day when I've walked enough
You'll show yourself through the mist.
Maybe…one day when I've been tried enough
Your comforting arms will hold me tight,
Your shoulders bear my tired head,

Your lips wipe off the past,
Your eyes will drink up my tears.

Maybe…
Maybe…I live for that day.
But now as I walk these miles alone,
I think of you.

CHAPTER 11

8 YEARS LATER

Eighteen is by far the most exciting age, a stepping-stone into adulthood but a giant leap into freedom. She was definitely going to make the most of it. Yes, seeking an undergrad in business studies was not an issue, fitting in with the hip-hop definitely was.

Having lived all her life in the oppressive Indian society but brought up to be a confident and self-assertive person, it was now time for Rhea Sud to live life on her terms. The only hitch was her sister Alia, Miss Prim and Proper, momma's perfect little girl. But she, Rhea, was daddy's spirited daughter and she had finally earned her way here. She was going to live life fully now - despite her sister. A trifle tentative and excited at the same time, she took a deep breath and made her way up the hallowed gates of The Virginia State University.

Alia, on the other hand, had her reservations. Yes, it was exciting but it was all so different and not what she had wanted. She was an Indian by every standard and she hoped it would not make her stand apart. She'd have any day settled for the local university back home where her friends were going to study. Anyway, she thought, if she stayed close to her sister she would hopefully not have to bother with being social herself. Her mother had insisted she go so far away, it would do her a world of good, she had said. She needed to gain more confidence, needed to be more independent. America was a long way from home;

in fact nothing about it was home. Not the food, nor the clothes, not even Ms Monica Vas, their local guardian. Gosh! She disliked her from the moment her mother had given them her brief background. Accepting her, thought Alia, would mean compromising on her own principles.

Autumn is one of the prettiest seasons in Virginia with a riot of coloured leaves in every hue of orange, purple, green, brown and yellow dancing in harmony on trees and then finding their way down on the ground as if in obeisance to winter. The girls found their way to the building that would house them for the next one year. A very modern structure with no distinctive feature that one could call exceptional, except for the chrysanthemums, which brought an explosion of life and colour to the otherwise nondescript place. The freshmen were arriving in a steady stream, parents and guardians in tow. Some were anxious and some excited, but all, without exception, thrilled to be there. Ms Vas had accompanied them too. She had promised to take care of the girls and take care she did. What a commotion she had created when she learnt that the girls had been separated and were to share their rooms with the other freshmen. She relented only when the girls, much to their embarrassment, pleaded with her to let them be, that they really preferred it this way. "Did they really?" thought Alia, but under the circumstances it was best to shut Ms Vas up, she'd made them look like incompetent, immature school kids in front of everyone. The sooner they settled down in their rooms the sooner would they be rid of her. Alia missed her mother now more than ever. How she wished her father had been well and then both of them and Aasma could have been here with them. But she understood even though she missed her dearly. She said a silent prayer for all of them.

It wasn't so with Rhea. She hated the mess Ms Vas had created but blamed her mother for it. Mother spent all her time with that kid, Rhea reflected. Weren't Alia and she her responsibilities too? Couldn't a nurse take charge of that brat just like dad was taken care of? She just did not give them the time they deserved. No, obviously they weren't important to her at all. Alia was a mummy's girl and so she still sucked up to her, but not Rhea. No way! She was as proud to be a Sud as she was to be her Daddy's girl. The stroke had left him a mere vegetable. She blamed her mother for this too. Everything was her mother's fault. But she, Rhea Sud, would correct things. Her degree would make her competent enough to take over all that was rightly hers, Sud Industries and the empire her father had built. She'd make it even bigger, so that one day when her father got well, and shc was sure in her heart that he would, he'd be so proud of her. So, while she was bid her time, she would make the most of what life dished out to her.

Alia was to share her room with a Pakistani and an African girl, Ulfat and Bobwana. Ulfat was shy and tentative about everything except when it came to her study area. She chose the corner table that had no windows but the largest shelf space. This suited Bobwana and Alia for they both got a window each. Some relief at least, Bobwana had said. Alia got to choose her bed, and she took the one closest to her desk, the other two did the same. This would be a compatible trio they all felt.

Rhea on the other hand was already in an ego battle. Her roommates Brigitte, a German and Sarah, a Canadian and she drew lots to allocate the desks and beds to make it all fair and square. Oh please, Rhea had thought this was so archaic, but Brigitte had insisted that this was the 'fair' way to do it and Sarah had played along too. So at the end of the draw Sarah was the only one with a desk by the window and a bed beside it. Since Brigitte would not let her exchange her window desk Rhea too refused to comply and hung on to the bed closer to Brigitte's desk. It was up to Sarah to keep the peace. She insisted they do the draws again and this time it was agreed that desks and beds went together. Brigitte had to settle for the windowless desk. Not even a day in school and Rhea had had her first scrap already.

The dorm-in-charge, a very matronly, middle-aged, Black American lady, made her rounds soon after the girls had settled in. The do's and don'ts were detailed and consequences made clear. A map of the campus was handed out to each one of them along with lecture schedules and the rooms they'd be conducted in. The third sheet provided the library, gym and swimming pool timings along with common entertainment room details. The girls were to attend the orientation with or without their guardians and then bid them goodbye. The welcome celebration in the evening was for the students only. All freshmen were expected to be in the dorm by midnight every night; the main door would then be locked. Any breach of this rule would have serious repercussions.

CHAPTER 12

Aakash increased the speed on the treadmill. He had been running for thirty minutes already and the last thirty would be at a level where he'd be aware of nothing else but the intense punishing physical pain. He prided his fitness at forty-two. It was the running that had kept him in peak physical condition and more importantly had kept his sanity intact.

Through the overlooking bay window he could see the freshman faulting and finding their way through the campus. He smiled as he remembered his first day here, completely lost and feeling very alien. The last ten years had changed all that and though he missed his land and its people, this was his life now and he loved being amongst these kids.

He checked the time on the wall clock, the Orientation was to commence after lunch and that left him ample time to soak himself in the soothing waters of the swimming pool before donning the formal attire of the custodian of the library. He was enjoying the water with lazy breaststrokes when he felt someone swim alongside him,

"Good morning, Dr. Ahmed." It was Ryan Brown from Physical Training.

"Morning to you too Ryan, and the PhD results have yet to come through, man, so hold the accolade for the moment." Aakash returned the greeting as they swam to the shallow end of the pool.

"Oh come on, I have no doubts about the result

and hats off to you, studying for a doctorate in Medieval History and working full time too." He exclaimed with both his hands in the air, "Boy-o-boy you're something else!"

Aakash became reflective, it had been an uphill task but the PhD had given him a purpose and the harder he worked his mind the better, the more pressure he put on himself, the better.

"Oh man! Get a load of that," said Ryan.

Aakash saw a beautiful young Indian girl, with a slim and strong body; make a perfect dive into the pool from the diving board. She surfaced halfway across the pool and then made strong freestyle strokes swimming to their end; she then turned herself underwater and continued swimming to the deep side.

"Wow!" whispered Ryan wide eyed.

"Wow what? Wow what a swimmer or wow what a babe?" Aakash asked knowing his friend.

"Wow both." Replied Ryan his eyes still affixed on her.

"Stop it pal, she's only a kid by the looks of her, and coach Murphy'll have your hide if he sees you ogling at her like this."

Aakash warned him trying to protect both Ryan's job and this lovely Indian girl.

"Hey, I know that big daddy," Ryan turned away from the girl, "but what a face, what a body and what a swimmer. Am I or am I looking forward to the new semester now." With that he hauled himself out of the pool and so did Aakash. They made their way to the changing room to get into their formals for the first programme on the agenda for the freshmen.

The Orientation was routine and had its share of speeches and introductions. American students were the majority joining this year too, but it was heartening to see a veritable number from other countries as well, especially the South East Asian countries. Patriotic as he was, Aakash took personal pride when he saw Indian kids excel.

The fraternity party followed where faculty was not invited to join but appointed to attend. They were expected to walk in and out at random to give the kids their space but maintain discipline too. It was here that Aakash spotted the same Indian girl who shared the pool with them that morning. She was sitting with a group of American kids, smoking and drinking like them. It was a visual assault and it took a definite effort on his part to continue normal behavior. Yes, all kids these days were very western in their ways, even though they came from essentially traditional cultures. His reaction was probably out of place, he felt, yet he made a mental note and decided to keep a watchful eye on this one. There was a strange familiarity to her face, but he just could not place her.

Scanning the room once again for any potential trouble he made his way to the coffee machine.

"Um . . .. excuse me sir, could you help me please?"

Aakash turned around with his cup of black liquid and he almost spilled it when he saw the young student seeking his help. She was an exact look alike of the indulgent Indian girl whom he'd just seen and it seemed to him he was looking in the face a ghost from his past. He turned to confirm the fact and then looked at the student in front of him.

"My twin sister," she said, answering the question he hadn't asked.

"Well, how may I help you?" he said pleasantly.

"This machine, I'm unfamiliar with it and I'm afraid I'll make a fool of myself." she replied smiling at her own helplessness.

He took to her instantly, "It's easy as a pie, come here let me show you. Okay, so what beverage would you like?"

"Does it serve Hot Chocolate?" she asked.

"It sure does, this is what you do. Place your cup here and press the button for hot water, and then look around for a packet of chocolate powder. Where is it? Ah! Here it is." He found it hidden in a corner.

"So all you have to do now is pour the contents into your cup and voilà!" He made a magician-like gesture with one hand as he offered her the beverage with the other.

"Thank you so much sir," she giggled, "you are very kind and friendly."

"Always around to help students thirsting for help. I'm Mr. Ahmed from the library." He smiled at his own wise crack and then shook hands with her.

"I'm Alia Sud." She smiled back.

"And your sister?" He wanted to know.

"Rhea, Rhea Sud." She replied.

"Hmm nice names, Alia and Rhea. I'll make a move now. Make friends, choose them carefully, and I'm always in the library during school hours if you require assistance."

"Yes sir, thank you."

He made his way to the door and turned to look at Rhea on his way out. She had noticed the interaction he had just had with Alia and was looking at him too. He raised his cup to her in greeting and was out of the room.

Rhea made a quick mental note. She'd seen him swimming with that handsome white guy and then again on the podium along side the faculty. What did he teach? Oh why was she not paying more attention? Anyway, he was by far the most handsome guy around here and an Indian at that. Yes, he'd be a trophy in her not so exciting life. The fact that he was faculty and so much older than she, was in fact quite the gauntlet she liked to pick up.

Alia's eyes followed him out of the room and she felt a pang of jealousy as she saw her sister score over her yet again where the attention of a man was concerned. There was something about Rhea that just drew them to her and she would use and then walked all over them. She'd never before envied her sister's charms, but now, at that moment Dr Ahmed became all-important to her. He was kind and had a sense of humour and had made her feel comfortable instead of stupid. He had treated her like a lady. She liked him and she would make him like her too, she decided, and most of all she would protect him from Rhea.

CHAPTER 13

College and campus life had slowly settled into their system. While the pressure of studies kept them busy, the everyday chores were less of a challenge now. How different life over here was and how even more differently did the two sisters react to it.

Alia's roommates were diagonally opposite. Ulfat was the studious type, not interested in extracurricular activities or making friends. She portrayed a quiet, introverted demeanor, though when in the room she relaxed enough to actually be one with the girls. Bobwana on the other hand was the coolest amongst the three. Nothing ruffled her and she took life as it came. Academics would take care of themselves, she maintained, she was more interested in sports, music and boys. She was part of the basketball team and was now trying desperately to get into the college band. Her natural style of dressing, walking and talking was so graceful and easy going that the company of boys seemed very natural too. Both Alia and Ulfat were in total awe of her and her control over the opposite sex, though neither envied her. It was fun at the end of the day, comfortably tucked in bed, to listen to her stories of how this boy tried to sweettalk her, and that one was rudely snubbed for trying to get too close. They would be hysterical with laughter for Bobwana had an incredible flair for the narrative. She was so genuine in her affection for the two of them too.

Rhea wasn't having that great a time. Having got off on the wrong foot with Brigitte, their relationship was always strained. Sarah was their buffer but there was precious little she could do with two strong-headed girls. Brigitte was a perfectionist and everything had to be just so. The room had to be perfectly in order, her study hours fixed and no power on earth could change that even if it meant staying up and studying by torchlight if the day had been demanding otherwise. Her closet was the classic example of order and her bed and desk neat to the T. It was for this very reason that Rhea got on her nerves even more for she was the exact antithesis. Rhea had never been used to doing her own domestic work. There had always been a personal maid to cater to her every need. Now she would wait for the laundry to pile high and then dump Alia with the needful. Her bed was left unmade and would be smoothed carelessly just before she crawled into it at night. Her desk resembled an organized mess. Brigitte was at the end of her tether and the more she nagged Rhea the more pleasure Rhea took in tormenting her. Sarah tried to intervene, but after a point decided it was best to let them fight their own battle.

"I'm going to report this mess to Ms Peters if it is not cleaned up," Brigitte threatened Rhea.

"What's your problem, woman? Do I tell you how to live your life?" Rhea retorted.

"That's because I do not go against rules," Brigitte replied very righteously.

"Oh really? And what if I tell everyone about you and Roxanne? Then what, huh? Or is that part of the rules too?" Rhea was very close to her and almost whispered the words into her face.

Brigitte's face went white. She was speechless. Roxanne, another German student, and she, had indulged in drugs in order to study longer hours. Then it was for recreational purposes too. Soon the addiction led to sex in order to obtain drugs. It was to Rhea's advantage that she had caught Brigitte redhanded.

"Think about it, girl, and learn to live and let live." With this Rhea gathered her books and stormed out of the room.

Rage was still seething strong within when she arrived for her economics lecture. What a creep – that girl! Why me? Why do I always get stuck with the weird lot? Immersed in her thoughts she missed the question Mr. Justin Orly had just asked of her.

Paul Smith her classmate sitting next to her nudged her, "Hey wake up."

"Huh?" She mentally returned to her present surroundings.

"Ms Sud, are you with us?" Mr. Orly had walked up to her.

"Yes sir," she replied.

"Good, then maybe you can throw some light on my query," he asked her gently.

"I'm sorry sir, but what was the question?" She sheepishly inquired.

"So you were not really with us, were you?" He was getting louder.

"I'm sorry sir, it won't..." she had started to apologize.

"Ms Sud, when you are in my class I expect your undivided attention, and that goes for all of you. If I have taken the trouble to prepare your lesson I expect your complete involvement too," he bellowed. "So now Ms Sud, in order to understand how much work goes into it, you will take the lecture next week and I shall sit, relax and day dream in your seat. Your topic is: 'The Comparative Study of European vs American Economics'. You will be speaking for forty-five minutes at the end of which you have to answer any questions the class throws at you." He looked at her with a smile of finality.

Not one to show any weakness, she looked him straight in the eye and said, "Yes sir."

"Good! So class, let's get back to today's lecture. Ms Sud, for your information, we were discussing The Essentials of World Economics."

Her cheeks were red with anger and embarrassment. How dare he humiliate her so? Back home she had been the darling of her teachers. Not only because all knew who she was and the generous donations the school received from her mother, but because she was an excellent student too. A regular topper in studies and sports, she had always taken pride in being the best. She would show them she was better than the best over here too. She would make Mr. Orly eat dust.

The lecture resumed and each and every student was listening with every ounce of concentration to avoid Orly's wrath. Rhea looked down at her book trying to hide the tears in her eyes. Paul slid her a note when Orly had his back to them. Surprised, she looked at him but he was looking straight ahead again; she opened it.

> He's a jerk; don't let him get under your skin. Can't you make that out? Imagine even his mother knew he was a dickhead, no wonder she called him Justin. Got that? Just-in … ha, ha, ha.

She smiled despite herself and looked gratefully at him. He was looking straight ahead but could see her from the corner of his eyes. He turned towards her and she mouthed 'thank you'. He gave her a quick wink and a nod of acceptance and then they were both a part of the extra attentive class.

Rhea could not wait for the day's classes to get over. She skipped lunch and went straight to the library. Five days to prepare a lecture she knew nothing about, but a lecture that in forty-five minutes would establish or destroy her forever.

The library at that hour was almost empty. She found an officious looking lady and approached her, "Excuse me, are you with the library?"

"Yes dear, you need assistance?" she replied, continuing to stack the pile of CDs in her hand.

"Yes please. I need all the reference material you have on European and American economics," Rhea requested.

"Economics, ok, let's see. This shelf here is our economics section. If you go through the contents you'll find what you are looking for." With that she walked away with the remaining pile of CDs that were waiting to be filed.

Wow, thought Rhea to herself, so different from the school library, where all you had to do was locate two reference books and the assignment fetched you an 'A' grade. There were several CD racks here; it would take her ages to get through it all. What the hell, she thought, in for a penny in for a pound. She pulled out the first five CDs that had America or Europe on them and sat herself down with her laptop. She selected at random anything that would make sense and copied it into her laptop. Soon the next batch of CDs was brought out and the process repeated on those too. The room was filling steadily with the post-lunch session of students and it felt good to be working hard amongst them. She decided to sort out what she had collected and then come back for more. Her heart skipped a beat as she walked towards the door, for in walked the handsome Indian teacher.

"Good afternoon," she wished him.

"Afternoon," he replied as they passed each other by.

Oh shoot, she thought to herself, this was a good chance to get to know who he was but she had no time to waste on trivial matters right now. He would have to wait.

CHAPTER 14

"Where have you been Rhea, I've gone crazy trying to locate you and why was your mobile switched off? Mom had called again; she wants to talk to you. Why can't you call back? What's your problem?" Alia was giving her a mouthful but she just kept silently sorting out her printouts.

"Rhea talk to me," she snatched the papers Rhea was sorting out.

"Give me those," Rhea yelled at her and tried to make a grab for them.

"No, not until you talk to me. Now tell me why the silent treatment for Mom?" Alia sat on Rhea's bed.

"Come on Alia, don't play stupid with me. You know how I feel about her. Now that I'm far away I don't have to suffer her any more. You are her pet and that Aasma is her life. As long as she takes care of my expenses I need nothing more from her. In any case it isn't her money that I'm using, its dad's. He earned it all. I owe her nothing. So why be a hypocrite and make a show of decency, for who's benefit?" Rhea looked at her sister. " Now give me my notes and tell her I'm fine when you speak to her. And also tell her to keep that Monica out of my hair, I can't bear the bitch."

Alia walked to the door and then turned around. "I feel sorry for you Rhea. We all love you, Mom, Aasma and I. Why can't you see that? Why are you so bitter? She's Mom, you understand? Mom. The only real parent we have. And she's struggling to keep Dad alive. Don't shut her out. You are not alone no matter how much you believe you are." And with that she slowly walked out of the door with her shoulders feeling very heavy.

"Damn!" Rhea cursed throwing the papers on her bed in frustration. She wanted to run away but there was no escape. She could never be far enough from her thoughts and memories and her mother who was the crux of it all. To make matters worse the terrifying assignment was getting nowhere.

She shut her computer and stormed out of her room heading straight for the swimming pool. She was midway through her punishing routine when Ryan entered the pool. He lazed through the lengths silently admiring her perfect body and amazing stamina. She swam the lengths and somersaulted under water to commence the next lap.

"Help! Help me please! Cramps. Help." Ryan heard her cry out as he entered the men's locker room. He ran back to the pool and dived in immediately. She was having a hard time staying afloat despite being a strong swimmer. By the time he pulled her to safety she was only semiconscious.

He slapped her face gently to wake her up and then rolled her onto her stomach to pump out any water she may have drunk. Her coughing was a relief and he rolled her onto her back again before tending to the cramps in her legs.

"You feeling better?" he asked her as he pulled both her feet to ease the cramps.

"Yes, thank you." She tried sitting up.

"That was a close call. Thank God I was here. I'm Ryan Brown, the assistant coach," he said helping her sit up against a wall. "Does this happen often, these cramps?"

"No, in fact this is the first time," she answered massaging her feet.

"Wait here, I'll get you a drink that'll make you feel better." With that Ryan was gone.

It gave Rhea time to catch her breath. It was a stupid thing she had done, swimming on an a stomach that had barely seen food in the last forty-eight hours, but she had to vent her frustrations somewhere and only ended up punishing herself.

Ryan was back " Here, this is an energy drink we give to our swimmers, I've spiked it with salt. Drink up." He commanded and she did as she was told.

"You're a new student, aren't you?" he asked.

"Yes, sir," she replied.

"Hey listen, call me Ryan," he told her

"Thank you, I'm Rhea." She extended her hand for him to shake.

"Hi Rhea, nice to meet you," he said, taking her hand. "May I ask you something?"

"Yes, of course," she replied.

"What was this fanatic swimming about? I was watching you; you hardly came up for air. You invited trouble you know." Then after a pause he added, "You've been crying; your eyes are swollen. So what is this about? Homesick already, or is something else bothering you?" He sat down too, leaning against the wall, and tipped the glass towards her face urging her to finish the drink. "You don't have to tell me anything you don't want to, but it's lonely so far away from home and I understand that," he continued.

She finished her drink and smiled at him, he was cute. "No Ryan, not homesick and yes something is bothering me." She swore him to secrecy and told him about Mr. Orly and her forthcoming ordeal.

He started laughing, "That old bastard, oops sorry, that was completely off the record too, ok?"

She smiled and nodded.

"Change up and come with me, Professor Ahmed is a good friend of mine and I'm sure he'll be able to help you." He stood up and taking her empty glass he extended his hand to help her up.

"Thank you." She was much better and the walking, though painful initially, made her feet feel normal once again.

He looked even more handsome and boyish with his clothes on Rhea observed. They walked to the library at an easy pace for her sake and the feeling was one of comfortable togetherness.

"Hey Doc," Ryan called out to Aakash.

"Hey Ryan," he imitated back.

"Doc, this is Rhea. Rhea this is Doc, I mean Professor Ahmed, Library Head of Department. Doc, Rhea has a problem." He related the entire story oblivious to the fact that both Aakash and Rhea were busy with their own personal thoughts.

So this is who he was. Professor Ahmed, Custodian library. He looked even more distinguished amongst his books - the guy Alia was sweet-talking. Now it was her chance to get under his skin.

All the while Aakash was trying hard to place her. Both the girls looked exactly alike. Maybe that was what triggered the feeling of familiarity about them, he thought. It was she who was partying with the kids and she now was already on the wrong side of Justin's wrath. He knew he was right about keeping an eye on her.

Ryan had completed his narrative and was excusing himself.

"I'll help her out Ryan." He discreetly gave Ryan a look that said 'I know what you are up to, pal.'

"Thanks Doc, owe you one." Ryan winked back equally discreetly.

"Thank you Ryan for saving my life twice over." Rhea smiled in gratitude.

"Go get 'em girl." He punched a fist into the air and went off.

"Ok, comparative study of European and American Economics. That's a little out of my league but I can help you with the suggested readings." Aakash started rummaging through the file index.

Rhea's heart sank, "I've already taken a few CDs but compiling them and preparing a lecture that'll knock Mr. Orly off his snug and pompous ass.... Oh my God! I'm sorry. I don't mean to be rude sir, honest. It's just that he humiliated me. Like he was this arrogant, white, all knowing professor ridiculing this stupid Indian girl. I swore to myself I would hit him where it hurt most; stump him in his own subject. But all I was able to find in the last two days was regular stuff, information anyone can access. I broke down because I know I'm going to make a fool of myself. I'll take what you suggest. I know my lecture will have the attention of the class, but once its over he'll finish me with his questions." She sighed and looked completely defeated.

Aakash was impressed. He'd never met anyone with such spirit of self-respect and defiance. Well aware of the fact that this was not only an attack of a personal nature but defined the way that prejudiced Orly, his impressionable class and perhaps even the entire college would come to view his country and its people, he felt patriotism stir strongly within him. He felt united with her in her fight against discrimination. "There has to be a way." He said looking at her in the eye.

"Sir?" She looked up at him.

"There has to be a way you can 'stump' the ol' chap. Let's do this together. Come on, I guess you are as raw at this as I am so being out league doesn't matter. Two heads are better than one." He pulled out a stack of CDs and divided them between the two. "You pull out relevant information from those and I'll do these. We'll meet tomorrow evening during prep and sort it out."

She couldn't believe her luck and was speechless.

"Go on girl, no time to waste." He encouraged her, "Let's do it, 'stump him'."

Not in a very, very long time – she could not even remember when she last felt so happy.

CHAPTER 15

It was the evening before the big day. Both she and Aakash had worked long hours and the lecture was finally ready. It was late and the library was empty except for the two of them and Ryan.

"Why don't you read it out aloud? Pretend I am Orly and there is a class full of students who may or may not be on your side. It'll help your presentation," Aakash suggested.

"Ok." Rhea walked to the head of the room and Aakash and Ryan moved to the back.

They had gone over the contents so many times that she knew it by heart. She sounded very confident and delivered a heartening performance. When she was done it was only Ryan though who applauded her effort. Both Aakash and Rhea knew it was thoroughly researched but still lacked the 'stump' material.

Aakash was about to say something to egg her confidence despite this when Alia came panting into the room.

"Rhea, thank God I found you. Sorry to interrupt sir. Rhea, Mom's called; she's on the line. Please come and talk to her," said Alia desperately.

Rhea's face showed the irritation she felt and both the men were taken aback.

Taking no regard of the presence of the others in the room Alia continued, "Please Rhea, it's Mom's birthday and she's in tears. Talk to her just this once, please."

Too embarrassed by her sister's melodrama she excused herself and took the phone from Alia and walked out of the room.

There was an uneasy silence amongst the three. No one knew the right thing to say.

Ryan was mesmerized by the similarity of their looks. Aakash was mentally remarking on the disparity of their personality.

He walked up to her and said, "Please convey our birthday greetings to your mother. She must miss you both dearly today. Rhea is very stressed about her presentation tomorrow. I'm sure…"

Alia broke down, "Even I don't know what her problem with Mom is. I've tried to go into the entire history of their relationship to find the answer. She loves Rhea so much but…"

Rhea returned almost instantly. Alia stopped short what she was going to say and hurriedly wiped the tears off her face.

One awkward moment too many - thought Aakash. "Let's quit for the day Rhea, you need to be fresh tomorrow."

The girls thanked the teachers and walked to their dorm. Through the library windows Aakash saw the girls have a heated argument as they walked back. What was it about these two that was so special, he wondered? What was the history that held all the answers? History in fact did hold several answers; his thesis in medieval history had been about that. It was yesterday's action that precipitated those of today. God knows what had occurred in the life of that child for her to be so bitter toward her mother. What secret in her history would solve her problems?

"History holds the answer," he repeated it aloud to himself.

That's it!

That was it; he knew where to find the 'stump' factor.

"Ryan, go call Rhea, bring her back this instant," he ordered.

"Doc…" Ryan started.

"Go boy go." Aakash practically pushed him out.

Every student in class was present that afternoon. No one wanted to miss the fun, Rhea thought. But she was more ready for this than she had been for anything else in her life and she couldn't wait to have her back at them.

She took her place in class and waited for Mr. Justin Orly to arrive.

Paul caught her attention, "Where have you been? I even chatted up your sister thinking she was you. Wanted to help you but was told you wanted to do this by yourself."

"Yeah, sorry."

"That's okay. Hey, all the best."

"Thanks," she accepted gracefully.

The class stood up as Orly walked in. She was deaf to all his rude remarks. He was going to be in her shoes soon and it had been his idea.

She took her stance and addressed the class, "The next forty-five minutes are mine. So no interruptions or questions or I will stop. The last fifteen minutes will be yours in which I will answer your questions, if you have any."

A single deep breath and she was rolling. One by one they all fell prey to the magic of her confidence and delivery. She was actually teaching them. Frantic notes were being taken when she told them to stop. She had made copies of her lecture and she handed each one a floppy as she walked around continuing with her lecture. She pulled a floppy out of her bag as she came to Mr. Orly, then stopped and looked him in the eye. Holding the floppy in front of him she then looked at the floppy and shook her head in the negative as though reminding herself that he didn't need this. Continuing with her verbal delivery she went ahead and gave it to the next student instead. An act that actually also signified that she was denying him a memento that she thought every one but he deserved. Where on the surface he could not fault her, since being the all-knowing teacher that he was, he would really have no need for it.

The class held their breath. Mr. Orly sat quietly in his chair. Forty-five minutes passed soon enough and the lecture was over. The class did not have many questions but Orly certainly showed his dominance. He first commended her on a well-prepared lecture and then bombarded her with pertinent and impertinent questions. She answered them all carefully, recalling the material she had studied in her research and reproducing it as though she was still taking class.

The fifteen minutes were finally over and with it her test. She did not need to hear the standing ovation her classmates gave her, the look of defeat on Prof Justin's face was enough. He walked up and shook her hand, "Congratulations Ms Sud, you have done yourself proud today. Please do take your seat once again."

As she walked up to her place she heard him talk to her back.

"Now Ms Sud, I hope you have learnt your lesson." The bastard, she thought to herself, he was so predictable. She was waiting for this moment when his larger than life ego would try to humiliate her again.

"Oh yes sir," she retorted back innocently. Then as if on the spur of the moment she had thought of something she said, " Sir, you have taken this lecture several times and I am sure you know it like the back of your hand."

"Well of course," he exclaimed with pride.

"So may I ask you a question that was bothering me?" she didn't wait for an answer but continued, "How did the history of these two great nations affect their economic policies where we see so many similarities in them during the medieval and ancient times?"

He was stumped. His hesitation was apparent to the entire class. Her timing was perfect. Before he could conjure some lame explanation she took out another set of floppies.

"That's ok Mr. Orly, it would give me great pleasure if you would accept this CD. It has my entire research on it.

"Why, thank you, dear," Mr. Orly managed in return, "And what did you say your name was?"

CHAPTER 16

It was a celebration. Aakash had invited both the sisters and Ryan to the pizza place within the campus. Alia, with Rhea's permission, had invited Paul too. He had been good to Rhea from the very beginning and was thrilled at the way she not only showed her brilliance but spirit too. Paul had been delighted at the invite and then surprised to find himself drawn to the quiet charm that was Alia. They had had a fun time re-enacting the expressions of each one in the class and were all in a happy and celebratory mood toasting to the 'stump factor'.

Rhea came back to the library with Aakash in the pretext that she had to prepare herself for Orly's next class, for he was sure to pick on her.

"Dr. Ahmed, the credit goes to you. If it weren't for your help I would have been destroyed today." She spoke with a certain amount of familiarity with him.

"You are over-reacting Rhea, with or without me you would have done well. No man is an island – remember this. We need each other. It is difficult to live alone and wrong to shut ourselves from others."

"This is about that phone call from my mother, isn't it?" she looked at him.

"Well, yes."

"It's best to drop that. It is something that I have to live with and cannot talk about." She said with absolute finality.

"Not with me perhaps, but if you can find someone

you trust you may just find that you might have exaggerated your reactions." He tried to council her.

"If there is anyone I could trust it's you," she gave him a warm and meaningful look that made Aakash a trifle uncomfortable, "but I know what I heard and saw and there is no changing that. Let it be, it's my baggage and I have been and will carry it to the end."

That was the end of that. She wasn't ready to expose her pain to anybody. It was the only way she could protect Alia. Aasma was innocent she knew, but that didn't stop her from keeping her distance from her. As for her mother, it was just as well Rhea was quiet for if she revealed what she had witnessed, each one of them would have been destroyed. Such was the trauma she had been carrying with her since she was nine years old.

"Ok Rhea, if ever you want to talk, you know where to find me."

"Thank you."

After a pause he added, "May I take the liberty of discussing one more thing?"

"But of course Professor Ahmed."

"Well, don't misunderstand me, but I saw you smoking a cigarette and enjoying your beer at the orientation party. Is that something you've done back in India too or…."

"No Professor, I did try the occasional cigarette at home, but that was on the sly behind a closed door and with friends. Over here it is a way of life and I don't want to stick out like a sore thumb." She confessed honestly.

"Is that a good enough reason to succumb to peer pressure? Surely your integrity, brilliance and tenacity should now hold you in high reverence amongst your colleagues. You know what I'm trying to say?" Aakash's voice had the gentle modulation of a coaxing friend and his words the admonishing of a parent.

She looked him straight in the eye, the seed of a genuine affection germinating in her heart. "I understand completely. Thank you."

He acknowledged it with an affectionate wink. "I have to leave for the airport now, Susan is arriving by the 10 o'clock flight."

"Susan?"

"You haven't met her, she's been on leave visiting her ailing mother in Scotland. The dance and drama teacher, my fiancé."

It was Rhea's turn to be at the receiving end of the 'stump factor'.

CHAPTER 17

1½ YEAR LATER

"You are coming with me to the airport on Monday." Alia informed Rhea.

Rhea was in the library, as usual, taking down meticulous notes. Susan's arrival had changed the equation she had shared with Prof Ahmed. It was only in the library that she could have him to herself. There were several other students in the library too, but that was different. As long as Susan wasn't around Rhea did not feel threatened. It wasn't as if the Prof had indicated in any way that he was interested in her more than he was toward any other student. But she enjoyed whatever time he would spend with her. He took interest in her academic life and seemed to care. Even the smallest of her problems was heard and an adult opinion proffered. There was precious little she could do about Susan but perhaps if she was around enough he would see how much better two Indians could bond albeit the years between them.

"No, I have a lot of work left. You go ahead. I'll meet Aasma later." She replied.

"But Rhea, Aasma is coming here for the first time. Don't you think …"

While Alia was reprimanding her decision a thought struck Rhea. If she did not go to the airport to fetch her sister, then she would have to go to Monica's house to visit her. That would be even more painful and a quick escape from there would be impossible. No it was better to go to the airport. All would be happy and she could make a rapid exit on one pretext or another.

"You're right, I'll come with you." She told Alia not taking her eyes off the computer screen. "So will you hire a car or will Monica come in her pay off?" She asked sarcastically.

"No dear, I'll hire a flying carpet. Of course Monica will fetch us on the way to the airport." Alia retorted back. She was relieved with Rhea's consent. Her mother had suffered enough already but to put their young and impressionable sister at the receiving end of Rhea's moods was unforgivable.

"Saving on fuel, hmm. Clever," Rhea played along.

"Talking in the library is prohibited girls." Aakash was passing them by and stopped as he heard their chatter.

Both girls stood up to greet him. Rhea was quicker to apologize.

"Sorry Prof, this sister of mine..."

Alia cut her short, "Our younger sister is coming to spend her summer vacations with us. I was coaxing Rhea to come with me to the airport. Thank God she's agreed." Aakash smiled at Alia's excitement even as she breathlessly continued in a loud whisper. " But you know the bummer Prof? She'll have to stay with Monica. I wish we could be together. I hate to think that the better part of her holiday will be spent with that...that..."

"Damian?" Rhea suggested.

It was a shocked Aakash who cut them both short. "Ok, enough. Let's meet up for another pizza dinner and sort this out. Just the three of us, ok?

What luck, what utterly brilliant luck, thought Rhea.

The pizza place was quite full but Rhea had gone well ahead and occupied the cozy corner table.

"So what's the deal here? Can I be party to this Monica business? Who is she and why do you dislike her so?" Aakash cut straight to the point.

The girls looked at each other and Alia spoke up. "It isn't something that we've discussed really, but both of us feel uncomfortable about Monica's life choices. We've seen our mother, completely devoted to her family, and here is a woman who, though married, thinks nothing about having an affair with a married man. He's left his wife and kids and she's hoping to marry him. That's it. We're both uncomfortable with that."

In that instant Aakash's thoughts took him back into that recess of his mind that he had, over the years, so desperately tried not to look at. He still had to learn how to think about her and not feel that deep yearning and urge to be with her as much physically as he did mentally. Learn to be able think about her and not feel the intense pain of separation and rejection. She had been a married woman too, married with children. An affair? Is that what it was? Not a commitment? Not some precious moments of life, stolen from life itself? What an ugly word that – affair. It reduced a relationship to a basic need; love spelt by three letters – s.e.x. No, for him it had been much more than an affair and for her - an affair perhaps? Would her girls have stood in judgement of her too? Would they have despised him for having loved their mother so completely? Rhea brought him back to the present.

"Mom said she had no choice but make her our guardian, Monica was a friend of hers from school and that we should not be so judgemental." Rhea offered. "When we came here we spent a week with her and were appalled at her attitude to life and people. She is so very cold and calculating, a conniving selfish woman. I'm sure Mom doesn't realize that her friend isn't the same as what she might have been. That's it."

"So have you told your parents about how you feel? You can change your local guardian, you know." Aakash suggested.

"Parents!" Aakash sensed the sarcasm mixed with pain in that. "Dad had a stroke several years back and has been lying almost comatose ever since." Rhea continued, "It's like we have and don't have a father."

Aakash absorbed this information; some of the pieces of Rhea's life were falling into place.

"And Mother - she can't see beyond her younger daughter and taking care of Dad's business." Rhea had let her pain and hatred surface yet again.

"That's not true Rhea. Mom's been very good to Dad and to us. You just don't let her come near you, that's your problem." Alia was almost angry with Rhea for showing their mother in such poor light in front of an outsider.

"There, there girls! Get a grip. Let's solve this Monica thing first," Aakash intervened.

"You want the sisters to be together, right? The best I could do for you would be to request Susan to house her. That way she'll be in the campus too and you will have easy access to her and the Monica factor gets eliminated. How does that grab you?"

Alia jumped at the idea and spontaneously kissed Aakash's hand "That would be just swell. Thank you Dr Ahmed, thank you so much."

He turned to seek Rhea's opinion, "Oh yes, that would be wonderful." She responded with pretence of gratitude. She envied the spontaneous show of affection that came naturally to Alia. To top that now she would have do be grateful to that Susan, and for what? Pay for someone else's sins?

Aakash called Susan and was very happy that she readily agreed to his suggestion. He knew she would. She was essentially a wonderfully warm and caring person. It was she who had cared enough to push their relationship ahead. She who had suggested they settle down. He could bank on her, he knew, but had learnt never to take anyone for granted.

"Oh that's great, if you'll excuse me Professor I'll go call Mom immediately and explain the change of plans to her." Alia sped off with that.

With just the two of them there Aakash decided to break the ice further.

"Very angry with your mother Rhea? She sounds like the quintessential Indian wife according to your sister. Why does Alia have to 'coax' you to fetch your sister and 'beg' you to wish your mother on her birthday? You are such a brilliant girl. Perfect in your very own way. But something is eating you from the inside and when it surfaces you are no longer a pretty person. You don't have to deal with it alone. I'm sure the problem won't look so bad once brought out in the open. Want to talk about it?"

Rhea sat very still looking at her hands placed on her lap.

"You know you can trust me. I'm not pushing you. I've tried to break through that wall of yours before. If you need more time, I can understand that."

What could she tell him that she hadn't told herself a million times before? She'd analyzed those lines in every which way she could and they told her the same thing. She had heard her father's voice coming from the library, angry and loud as never before. She'd slowly crept to the door and looked through the keyhole. Her father's fury had been directed at her mother, she could see and her mother was crying. It was her mother's words that fell on her ears, '*No, this baby may not be yours and that is your punishment.*' She had heard her say those exact words. Then that terrible scene unfolded before her eyes once again. That of her father picking up the table lamp and hitting her mother hard across her face and then collapsing too. She remembered being so frightened at that time that not a sound had escaped her. She had stood up from her crouched position by the keyhole to open the door. Even at nine years she knew her world would never be the same again. That she was opening the door to secrets and deceit and she would have to carry them alone.

She could not bring herself to speak about it.

"It's ok, if you aren't ready now. Take your time." Prof. Ahmed was talking to her.

She looked up at him wanting to desperately confide in him and have him share that special bond with her. But she could still not bring herself to talk about that night, the night that changed her life.

The tears in her eyes said it all and he understood. She got up to leave and thanked him for dinner and his help.

"Rhea wait a second, what did you say your sister's name was? Susan will need to know." He asked her.

"Aasma."

His heart skipped a beat, a simile for his name, he thought. Could it be…? No way, and he shook off the cobwebs of his past from his thoughts.

CHAPTER 18

"Bobwana, wake up." Alia whispered into her ear.

"What…"

"Shhh, quiet." Alia silenced her. " Ulfat is not in her bed. I think she's in some kind of trouble."

"What time is it?" asked Bobwana, reaching for her watch.

"It's 2.30 in the morning. I heard Ulfat crying into her pillow last night and now she's missing. Where do you think she is?" Alia asked her.

"I don't know, maybe in the loo."

"No, I went to use the loo myself, she isn't there." Alia replied.

"Shoot! We'll have to go look for her." Bobwana got out of bed quickly. "Where could she go at this hour? Why didn't you tell me she was crying?" Ulfat had shared a special bond with Bobwana. Alia felt really bad about not reading more into those tears.

"I … I thought she must be homesick or something. Do you think it is something to do with Irfan?" Alia looked questioningly at her roommate.

"It might just be. You suppose she's sneaked off to the boys hostel? Jesus! What a stupid thing that would be." Bobwana said as she dressed hurriedly.

"So what shall we do? Wait for her to come back or go look for her?" Alia was confused herself. If they went looking for her and were caught they would be in serious trouble and yet if they did not, well she would return sooner or later and they would then sort out any mess their friend was in. "Let's wait for her to come back, I mean she will sooner or later. We don't even know where she is."

"Tell you what, girl, you wait here and I'll go to the boy's dorm to look for her." She'd been to the boys dorm often enough and was therefore more confident. "Beep me on my pager if she arrives before I do. I had warned her that Irfan fellow was up to no good, but she was smitten. They had gotten married, she told me. Something to do with saying the word 'Nikah' three times in front of his no-good friends."

"Nikah? Oh my God!" said Alia, but before she could react further Bobwana jumped out of the window and was on her way.

The clock on her desk kept ticking the seconds away. There was no sign of the girls and a very nervous feeling started in the pit of Alia's stomach. Ulfat and Irfan had got married? Good God! She hadn't even known about it. Ulfat knew that Bobwana and she disliked Irfan. He had made passes at both of them and wasn't the type who would be loyal to any single relationship. Of late he had been his charming best towards Ulfat and she had fallen madly in love with him. She could just not see what was so obvious to the rest of them. What a stupid girl, Alia thought, and prayed Irfan would keep his word and not break her gullible and naïve friend's heart.

She wanted desperately to page Bobwana to find out what was taking her so long. She alternately paced the room, peered out of the window and prayed. Very slowly, the clock ticked the long night away and finally the morning sun hit the campus. In order to look inconspicuous and like one of the joggers, Alia wore her shorts and sneakers and went on a sprint in the general direction of the boy's dorm. She'd barely covered half the ground when she noticed a lot of commotion near the school office. She knew in her heart this had something to do with her roommate.

Loud sirens disturbed the early morning air. An ambulance and two police cars had pulled up at the office. The Dean himself was present at the porch to meet them. He shook their hands and then they all sat in the car and drove off. Alia ran behind the speeding car, knowing something dreadful had happened and prayed for the safety of her friends. Panting and completely out of breath she pushed her way through the crowd. She did not know what to expect but when she finally managed to break through the crowd she stood stunned. Ulfat had been stabbed in the stomach and lay deathly still with her eyes half open. Bobwana sat beside her with silent tears rolling down her cheeks. She had blood all over her and was being arrested without any resistance on her part. She was like a zombie, completely in a trance.

"… You have the right to remain silent. Anything you say or do, can and will be held against you in the court of law…"

"Wha…" she seemed to have woken up with those words, "what are you doing? Why are you arresting me? I haven't done this. It's Irfan. Arrest him." She pleaded with them. Then she spotted Alia. "Alia! Alia! Thank God you're here. Tell these people I'm innocent; they think I've killed Ulfat. Ulfat was my friend Alia; you know that. Tell them how I came looking for her. Alia!" She heard Bobwana's desperate voice filter into her eardrums as she collapsed onto the grass.

Consciousness returned to her in the ambulance. Her strange surroundings scared her. Still in a state of shock, she screamed and started thrashing her arms trying to remove the intra-venous needle from her body.

"Let me go, let me go, who are you?"

"It's ok love, it's ok. We're taking you to the hospital. You'll be fine." The paramedic tried to comfort her but she fought back with all her strength begging them to let her go.

"No, no I don't want a shot… please I have to find my friend… Ulfat… ohhh…" The sedative took effect and she slipped into a deep drug-induced sleep.

When the medication wore off and she opened her eyes again she was equally lost and petrified to find herself in the semi-darkened hospital room. Using all her strength she tried to get up. *I have to run away. Horrible things are happening over here. I have to escape; they'll get me too. Escape. Run.*

"Alia, what are you doing?" she heard the familiar and most welcome voice of Dr. Ahmed and turned to see him.

He had been sitting beside her bed and immediately reached for her when he saw her sit up so suddenly. She was so very relieved to see him. *She would be safe at last; he would protect her from them all.* She just wrapped her arms around him and cried.

"Take me home, I don't want to stay here anymore, I want to go home. Please, I want to go to my mother. I want to go home. I don't like it here… Ulfat, oh my God, Ulfat…she's dead. Dead. So much blood… Oh my God…Ulfat…why didn't you listen to us…Bobwana …innocent... Bobwana… innocent." She slumped unconscious into his arms.

Aakash just held her and let her cry. She had gone through a ghastly experience and the trauma of shock could wreck her for life if it wasn't handled with care. He was angry as hell at the authorities for sending her alone to the hospital. They could have waited for her sister or even sent a friend of hers along. They had argued that it had been too early in the morning and it was an emergency; none of the students were aroun. The paramedics and police had taken over the situation and everything had happened too fast. Mr. Francis, the Dean, had insisted they take Ulfat's body away as soon as possible; he did not want the other students to witness and suffer what Alia had. If Alia's condition worsened her parents could easily sue the university for irresponsibility.

It was Ryan who called up Aakash. The Gym was the first facility to go operational early in the morning. Ryan reached the scene of the crime whilst the forensic personnel were still at work. He had called Aakash and given him all the gruesome details and told him that Alia had been rushed to the State Hospital in an unconscious state.

Aakash decided to go to the hospital immediately and had instructed Ryan to bring Rhea and Susan there too. Susan was a quick after thought, in case he needed her to help with the girls. He would see to all the arrangements regarding Alia's care personally. It had been difficult explaining his relationship with the girls to the school authorities, but Ryan had been a great help on that score too.

Rhea had reacted most unexpectedly on reaching the hospital. He thought she was a strong girl but she had broken down and was hysterical when she saw Alia. An I.V. drip and various leads were monitoring Alia's vital signs. Once Rhea calmed down he had sent her with Ryan to collect their younger sister from the airport and to bring her to the hospital. Thank God for Ryan, he thought. Their local guardian, Monica, was unavailable. When contacted at her workplace they were told that she had been admitted to a clinic for treatment.

He gently laid Alia back onto the bed. Susan was present in the room with him but Alia had not even seen her. He called the nurse in and left her to do the needful while he went to make a call to the Dean.

"Alia didi, can you hear me? Wake up please, Alia. Open your eyes didi." *Deep in her sleep she could hear a familiar voice from her past calling her. It was very faint and echoed in her ears. Wake up it said; wake up. She had to open her eyes, the voice was telling her so. Slowly, very slowly the sweet voice became louder and clearer and much more closer. Yes, she knew that voice; it was Aasma's. Aasma wanted her to open her eyes. She was home. Now she would be safe. She would open her eyes, for Aasma she would open them.*

"Alia didi, can you hear me? I'm Aasma. Your Aasma. Please wake up." Aasma had been pleading by her bed as she had been for the last two days, ever since she had arrived. Alia had slipped into coma, a consequence of the shock. The girls were terrified. They had seen their father vegetate for the better part of their lives and to see Alia lying so still was the last straw. Their mother had been called in and she was arriving the following morning.

Aakash was taken aback when he saw Aasma walk up the hospital corridor with Rhea. He knew now what it was about the twins that made them so special to him. Aasma had come as a complete surprise. She was the spitting image of her mother, a little Amrita. What a small world, he thought to himself. First fate had brought the mother into his life and then taken her away. Then her daughters held a special place in his heart and he could not explain why. Finally along came little Aasma. She had named her daughter Aasma after him, he knew. It was small relief for his ego that had suffered endless days of pain waiting for word from her. She would be arriving soon. Amrita would be arriving soon. My God, after all these years he never dreamt that he would ever meet her again and not like this for sure. He remembered the last time he looked forward to meeting her. It was when she was coming to Jammu to meet him. Their time together flashed through his mind. What would it be like to meet her after all this time? How well had she worn these years? Had she thought of him at least half as often as he had dreamt of her? Would she be as thrilled as him to meet again? Would she? Or...? No. He could not let her see him. She had her life and he was not a part of it. She had made that clear with that one mail. Besides which, he would not be able to see her anguish over her child. Oh dear God, so it was her husband who was in coma. Now her Alia was so critical. It was she who was at the receiving end of Rhea's wrath. What was the story of Amrita's life? She had suffered more than he did in so many more ways. He almost felt guilty about being angry with her for hurting him.

Anyway, she was arriving soon and arrangements for boarding and lodging had to be made. The Dean had offered the official college guesthouse that hosted university guests to them for as long as it would take Alia to recover. Aakash was sure though, like Aasma and Rhea, even Amrita would station herself at the hospital. Susan would take Rhea to the airport, he decided. Seeing Ryan and Rhea together might startle Amrita, he was sure Rhea had told her mother nothing about her relationship with Ryan.

Aasma's desperate pleas brought him back to the present.

"Alia didi." Aasma was holding her hand and crying.

His heart went out to this child. She had refused to leave her sister's bedside and kept calling out to her, trying to wake her up.

"Come dear, we must leave now." Susan tried to coax her off the bed.

Someone was taking her Aasma away from her. Wait! Don't go away Aasma, please. I will open my eyes...open my eyes...open eyes; she commanded herself, ... open eyes. Can't let Aasma leave me. Aasma wait for me. Wait for me. Wait! Aasma...

"Stop." Aasma held Susan away. "Rhea didi, come here quick."

Rhea had been sitting with Ryan, Paul and Aakash outside the room and they all came running in.

"Rhea didi, look." Aasma pointed towards her hand. Alia was holding on to it so tight that her knuckles had turned white.

There was a flood of relief in the room and each one of them started calling out to Alia to come back to them, to wake up.

Aasma wait...I'm coming with you...don't go...open eyes... open eyes; she told herself...if you want your Aasma you have to open eyes...NOW!

She was the first person Alia saw, sitting on her bed and holding their hands to her heart, her Aasma.

"Alia didi?" Aasma said in disbelief.

Very slowly, as if she was saying words for the first time, Alia smiled and said, "Aasma. My Aasma."

They all hugged each other and cried tears of relief and gratitude.

CHAPTER 19

"It's ok mom, you don't have to fuss over me anymore, I am fine." Alia said in a voice that was still fragile with the aftereffects of the shock and medication.

"I'm so sorry darling; I should have kept you girls with me. I thought this college experience in the USA would help you, but instead.... I'm taking you both back with me," Amrita declared. Alia had not seen her mother so upset in a long time.

" Mom, I love it here and so does Rhea. We're half way through the third semester. You cannot freak out over this. I will be absolutely all right here. Please, now stop it, you're making me nervous."

Amrita took a long hard look at her daughter and said, "You're right, life's experiences have to make us stronger. We must not run away from them. On the contrary, if we look trouble in the eye, we somehow tame it. I'm proud of you, my darling. Coming here has in fact done you good. You are now my big girl. " She kissed her daughter's forehead. "Give me a moment, I have something to show you." She went to her room and came back with her diary.

"Alia, years back, when I was in school, the girl who sat next to me in class died of kidney failure. It was a horrible shock. It was also the first time that I had to deal with death. I was angry, sad, alone and confused. I had a conversation with death - on paper, and it helped my healing process. It helped me to understand death. I would like to share it with you today," Amrita said to Alia.

"Read it out to me, mom," said Alia, her voice shaking a little as she did.

Amrita opened the diary to the appropriate page and laid it before Alia. She recited the poem and Alia's eyes scanned the words in tandem with her mother's recitation.

An Address To Death

Death you are so untimely,
You are so selfish, so impolite,
You do not wait nor ask,
You have taken from me
what was mine – never yours.

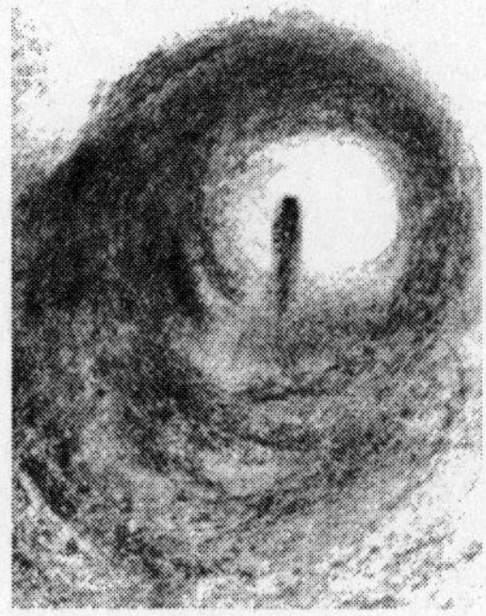

Do you not have feelings?
Do you not see the sorrow you
 cause –
that you are responsible for?
Do you not feel for the
 bereaved?

Your consolation lies in that
What you have so rudely
 snatched from me__
You will take care of,
You will bless,
I rest in that.

Yet, what will fill the void in my heart?
The emptiness of my existence?

Time will heal all wounds indeed!
But will it be so knowing__
All that I love will be yours,
All that loves me will be yours,
That you will again and yet again

Spread your dark shadow on my fate,
Make me bow to you in vain?

My tears I cry in self-pity,
In the knowledge you won't be moved.
My tears I cry for all bereaved,
For all I have to lose.

But think not you have won over me,
Your victory is your failure.
For those I love I do with my soul,
That love you cannot take,
That love and my memories will pull me through,
Guide me through each day.

That what is mine is immortal,
That what is mine you cannot take.
That what is mine is immortal,
That what is mine you did not take.

Amrita finished reciting the poem. Alia read it once again before shutting the diary and handing it back to her mother.

"Thanks mom, for sharing that with me. I understand it. I can see the anger, the grief and the confusion and can feel where the healing came from." Alia spoke softly, on the verge of tears.

Amrita held her daughter close to her heart.

"Mom, is your classmate still alive in your heart?"

"Isn't Ulfat still alive in your heart?" Alia nodded, her silent tears flowing unchecked. "And she will always be, my child, as long as you remember her she will be alive."

She had felt Alia tense at the mention of Ulfat's name. "Deal with it Alia, and when you are ready, come to me and we'll remember our friends together."

Alia nodded her reply once again.

Amrita returned to her chores. "Where are your sisters?" she asked. Amrita had been cooking all the Indian fares that the girls enjoyed. Lunch was waiting hot and delicious on the table.

The guest apartment on the campus, offered to them by the Dean, was a relief to all. For one, they could stay together and the twins could attend classes too. Also, Alia had to attend a daily group therapy session at the campus clinic till she was mentally in control of herself. She had nightmares and woke up in a sweat or even screaming, as she had done the previous night. She had learnt to push the dreadful events away into a far corner of her brain during the day, so far that she could pretend they no longer existed.

A ring of the doorbell made Alia jump in her chair. Amrita noticed this and smiled back reassuringly as she went to open the door. A handsome young American stood holding a colourful bouquet of flowers.

"Hello, I'm Paul, Paul Smith." He extended his hand in greeting. "You must be Alia's very beautiful mother. Is she all right? May I meet her?"

"Hello, yes I'm Alia's mother and thank you for the compliment."

She said as they shook hands. "She's better. Just wait a moment please." Amrita returned quickly and asked Alia if she would like to meet a Paul Smith. The way her daughter's face lit up was answer enough; nevertheless she waited for a formal confirmation.

"Oh yes mom. Wait! Do I look ok? My hair, is it a mess?"

"You look beautiful darling." Amrita beamed back.

Her baby had grown up and was in love, even if she wasn't aware of it. This was perhaps the best medicine for her right now. The unpredictability of life was a certainty therefore each moment of life had to be lived in all its glory. She had full confidence in her kids and wanted them to make their own choices in life. To be given a chance to make your own mistakes and triumph in your victories, that was what she had been denied. She went to the door and opened it once again, "Do come in, Alia is in the lounge."

"Thanks."

She watched him enter and heard the excitement in Alia's voice as she welcomed him. She thought it best to respect their privacy and so from the door itself she shouted out to Alia, "I'm going for a short walk kids, be back soon."

"Right mom," Alia answered back

Paul came to the door to meet her, "You enjoy your walk Mrs. Sud, I'll take care of Alia till you return."

"Don't talk to her about Ulfat," Amrita warned him.

"I won't, don't worry." He reassured her.

"Ok, good, thank you." Amrita quite out of the blue felt a trifle insecure, like she wasn't needed, and it showed.

He sensed this. "My pleasure, Mrs. Sud." Then on impulse he hugged her, "You go take a break, you need it."

The February chill was refreshing. She had been cooped up in the apartment for a week. The hospital had released Alia knowing she would be much better off with her mother. Now that her daughter was getting better and stronger by the day Amrita could actually take time off to appreciate the fact that she was in the States. This was the first time she had left Rahul for anything else besides work and she felt free. She wasn't sure how long Alia would need her here but she would stay for as long as it took to make sure her child would be absolutely all right on her own. She only prayed Rahul would hold on.

Away from Rahul and not feeling guilty to be so, she wanted to make the most of this unexpected freedom. It was a good thing she was wearing her sneakers and tracksuit. She started a slow and comfortable jog into the university gardens. This was life, she thought, as she savoured the freshness of the air. Feeling light hearted, she wondered why she didn't allow herself this freedom on a regular basis? Why she had caged herself in a cocoon like existence. Some day her girls would need her even less, what would she do with her life then? How much longer was Rahul going to live? How much longer were they both going to be punished? And what kind of life would there be for her after Rahul was no more? What kind of a life did she have with him alive, whether now or even before? She decided to banish these depressing thoughts and tried to absorb the beauty of the place. Who was that kind gentlemen the girls spoke of so fondly? Ah yes, Professor Ahmed. She wished she could meet him and thank him personally for all that he had done. He had told the girls to spend time with their mother and sister, that he had a lot of catching up to do at the library and would not be able to visit them. Such a shame, she thought. Perhaps she could visit the library herself sometime. Yes, that would be the right thing to do. Maybe she could ask Rhea to take her there. Or maybe she could ask directions and go meet him herself. Why not? Rhea may not be too happy doing her a favour. Thank God she was friendlier towards Aasma now. She took her shopping and also let her hang around with her when she was not attending lectures. Even today, being Sunday, they had had breakfast and Aasma had left with Rhea saying they'd be back in time for lunch and thereafter to challenge anyone to a game of chess. It was a pleasure seeing Aasma delighting in this show of affection. She would visit Prof. Ahmed herself, the library was open on all days she had been told and now was as good a time as any.

CHAPTER 20

The huge expanse and grandeur of the library took Amrita's breath away. She was glad that her girls had had an opportunity to study in such a beautiful environment. Infact it's impressive elegance made her feel inappropriately dressed. Bad idea, she said to herself, coming here on impulse. At the time she had felt her casual attire was acceptable in the unassuming campus atmosphere and especially on a Sunday. But now she saw clearly the error of her judgment. Turn around Amrita, she told her self, and come back again dressed more like Mrs. Sud. Walking back slowly she allowed herself time to admire the imposing aisles neatly stacked with leather bound reference books and compact discs. The shelves ran very tall and beautiful sliding wooden ladders helped access the topmost shelves. She was admiring one such ladder and the agile and lithe body who had climbed up to its uppermost rungs. He was a good ten feet above the ground and yet looked so comfortable studying a book up there. She looked up at him as she walked by and then she froze. It couldn't be. Her eyes were deceiving her. He was in Jammu. This had to be a lookalike. But she just had to turn around and confirm the resemblance for herself once more. With her heart pounding in her ears she turned to look at him. He was still reading the book but when she stopped abruptly and turned to look at him he too looked down at her by moving his eyes above the reading glasses. Complete disbelief at what he was seeing was apparent on his face. He removed his glasses and waited for her to make the first move.

To an onlooker it would have seemed like a 'still' from a movie frame. They stood looking at each other for so long.

There were no thoughts running through her mind, she could hardly even hear her pounding heart. There was only one name that completely encompassed her and held her in its spell: Aakash.

He stopped breathing when he realized it was she. And when she turned around to look at him there were several things he wanted to do at the same time. Run and hide and protect both of them from any more pain. Ask her why she loved him and left him, why she used him so? Make her feel all the pain, hurt and humiliation he had felt. Hold her in his arms and take all her troubles. Hold her in his arms; bury his face in her hair and never let her go. But all he could do was stand atop the ladder and just look into her face.

He had cleverly hidden behind the secure wall of work. The girls had bought his story about work backlog. He'd promised himself he would stay away from Amrita, that he wouldn't allow himself even a glimpse. No rekindling of old emotions, no more heartache he had promised himself and it had been so. She was living in the same campus as him and that was enough to make very cell in his body come alive. 'I will love you for as long as the skies exist. I will love you for as long Aakash.' He had wanted to believe those lines from her poem so desperately. Wanted to believe she still loved him. That was when he realized the truth. The only reason he wanted to believe that was because no matter how far back in his mind he had pushed and tried to forget her, she was still the only woman he loved and he loved her dearly even till this day. Poor Susan, poor adorable, loving Susan. It was she who had helped him live a normal life these last few years. She had wanted this marriage. He would have to break her heart. He couldn't let either of them live a lie, they both deserved better than that. He would find the right time and break it to her gently; the time had not arrived as yet. He needed to feel committed to her, to hide behind this relationship so that he could keep away from Amrita. It didn't matter how he felt about Amrita, he knew how she felt about him. Now that he knew even more about her, the last thing he wanted was to complicate either of their lives any further than it already was. No fresh memories to weep over when she left. He would stay away and aloof.

He climbed down and stepped off the ladder and now that they were face to face he could see a film of water in her eyes that she quickly blinked away.

"Hello Amrita. Surprised?" he said.

"Aakash?" she said still not believing her eyes.

He was quiet for a while letting her absorb the fact, he knew the shock he had felt when realization had struck home. In any case he was deciding how he would play-act his role now that they had met, he was buying time.

With a twinkle in his eyes he replied, "Actually Tom Cruise, I'm using Aakash's guise to keep the girls away." He replaced the book and climbed down the ladder.

His same old mischievous self she thought, and it felt so good to hear it. "It won't work."

"How are you Amrita?" he asked her genuinely wanting to know.

"Fine, and you?" she asked him back.

"Oh fine too, absolutely fine." He realized he might have sounded a little too emphatic there, as though he was proving a point, so he added, "I love my work and the kids. I'm glad I decided to leave Jammu."

That was right, she recalled that he had shifted to the USA, but that he was here was too much of a co-incidence. Did he know that Alia and Rhea were her daughters or was she still 'Amrita from Delhi' for him? It didn't matter now after all these years and with her life as it was even if he knew her real identity; she was now in control of it.

"I'm happy for you. I, umm... I had come to meet a Professor Ahmed," she said to him. He smiled at her again without saying a word and on seeing his smile it all fit in place. "But of course, Aakash Ahmed. Oh my God! What a co-incidence. Who would believe it? You've come a long way Aakash. Congratulations. Rhea and Alia Sud are my girls."

"I know, I realized as much when I saw Aasma. She has very little of her father in her."

Amrita's face lost colour, how much of himself had he seen in her?

"Aasma, hmm, very pretty, I wonder who chose that name?" He knew he was treading on dangerous ground and should stop, but he wanted her to acknowledge his influence in her life. Subconsciously he also wanted to hurt her like she had hurt him.

"My husband." She lied looking him in the eye, not knowing where this conversation was going.

"Ah, good taste – your old man, I've always maintained that." He smiled, "Tell me Amrita, had it been a boy would your husband have named him Amber perhaps?" But without waiting for her to reply he started laughing, " Hey I'm only kidding, don't look at me like that."

She knew that he knew, but he didn't know the whole truth.

"Come and join me for a cup of coffee. I'll be honoured." He invited her into his office.

She had no choice but to follow him there, he was after all the man who had taken care of her critically ill daughter. She hadn't even started thanking him for that. It would seem ungrateful and rude if she declined his offer.

Like the library, this room too did Aakash's status proud. The rosewood desk with green leather and gold pin tuck finish was stately and elegant. There was no family portrait adorning it and she wasn't about to question his love life, so to distract her thoughts she looked around noticing the other furbishing details. The high chair was upholstered in the same green, red and gold as that of the curtains, only the chair was greener and the curtains had more red. A small fire kept the room warm and cozy. Books were spaced with bonsai cacti and miniatures of antique cars in a bookcase that lined two intersecting walls. Two large chairs and a round table found their place along with tall palms and a standing lamp in the adjacent corner of the room. The corner on the left of his table boasted of a standing dated upright bronze statue of a Chinese warrior replete with full armour, aiming toward the centre of the room with his arrow. The corner on the right held Aakash's jacket and tie. The walls were veneered and the flooring had a warm dullish red carpet. A large Picasso painting with an ornately carved frame hung majestically on the wall behind his desk. The full-length curtains had been drawn open and the afternoon sun came flooding in through the French windows that opened onto a spacious balcony. The balcony too was an artistic conglomeration of ferns, flowers, and fruits.

"It's beautiful." she remarked.

"It is," he said looking at his plants; he did not want to send any message that might be misconstrued. "As you can see I've tried to bring some of my country home effect into this formal office setting."

She walked to the bookshelf. "Those are very valuable books, some of them date back to the fifteenth century. Restorers come in to dust and maintain them." He informed her as he poured the coffee. "It was these books that inspired me to take a doctorate in medieval history."

"You've been busy," she said sipping her coffee. She sat down and placed her cup on the table hardly noticing the intricate inlay work on it. "Thank you Aakash, for all that you've done for my girls. They claim you've saved both their lives. They are twins and Rhea was only half alive, she says, while Alia was in coma. She is a very different girl now. You've spent some time with them, I know, so you will be able to mark the change. She's calmer and a little more reasonable but most of all Aasma, whom she hardly spoke to before, seems to have become her favourite." She picked up her cup again and stirred its contents with the spoon looking straight down at it. Aakash was quiet, she wanted to say something and was gathering the courage to do so. He let her take her time.

"I have not had a very easy life. The girls, all three, they mean the world to me. I would never do anything to harm or hurt them. Never." She was still looking at her coffee. He was leaning against his desk; both hands loosely folded on his chest, the coffee mug in his right hand, looking straight at her. It gave him an opportunity to see her gorgeous face after so many years; also he was very curious to find out what was on her mind.

"You and me Aakash." *OK here it comes whatever it is, he thought.*

"The girls must never know." She still did not look up.

What did she think he was? He walked up to her, put his coffee mug on the table and sat on his haunches facing her, "Amrita, goddamit, what's wrong with you? Don't you know me even that little much? Jesus! I can't believe you even said something like this. What did you think I was going to do? Tell those vulnerable teenagers that I had had an affair with their mother the next time I bumped into them? Good God Amrita, I have been trying to hide 'you and me' from *me*." She was looking at him as he spoke, but his last few words took her breath away. He saw the look in her eyes. The words had slipped out and were not meant as she had understood them, but trying to explain any further would be like walking on quicksand. So he just stood up and walked to the French windows in complete exasperation. Running his fingers through his hair he looked out abstractly shaking his head in denial.

"I am grateful Aakash, for all your help and for your word of honour. I appreciate it." She said very quietly as she put her cup down and stood up to leave.

"Wait Amrita." *Wait don't go, not yet, not like this,* he wanted to say. "I have to come and talk to Alia. I've been commissioned by the Dean's office to officially escort Alia through this ordeal. The court hearing is coming up soon and I have to break ground with her. Your meeting me like this is a blessing. I wasn't sure how I would have handled it - dealing with your daughter and avoid meeting you at the same time. Don't look so shocked Amrita, it was only so that you would not be put in an awkward situation." He saw her visibly relax with that last consoling line. "I'll come along with you." He knew this was lunchtime and he was imposing on her but his words had cut through her being, he had seen it in her eyes. He wanted to kick himself for reacting so. Maybe he could take the edge off them by spending some more time with her; making her laugh perhaps - she had always loved his humour. Her life was difficult enough without him adding to it. In any case the Bobwana case had to be talked about too. Alia had to face the truth.

He didn't wait for her consent and collecting his keys he shut the door behind them.

They walked to the guesthouse, both were quiet initially absorbed in their own thoughts. The words 'hiding you and me from me' were hanging like a noose around both their necks. What did he mean by that, thought Amrita. That he was desperately trying to forget their time together, of course. You desperately want to forget bad memories or a mistake perhaps. Oh dear God, she was his mistake and he a living truth in her life. She could only thank God she had not written to him again after that one mail and made a bigger fool of herself. She must never let him look too deep into her eyes for they were a complete give away. Her Aakash had been with her all this while, in her heart and in front of her eyes, and would remain there. This man, walking beside her, was a stranger and did not have the power to hurt her. Her Aakash worshipped the ground she walked on. This man she did not know nor did she want to.

Aakash knew she was fretting over his words and he had to distract her.

"You OK?" he asked her softly.

"Yes." was her curt reply.

Damn! Think of something else Aakash, he said to himself.

"Do you still run as fast as you did?" he asked. He had noticed how well maintained and gorgeous she looked. The pink and gray tracksuit and sneakers prompted that opening line.

"I still run." Her reply was curt.

"I bet I can beat you now, I've been running every day

too. Want a match?" he smiled his old familiar smile where one corner of his lips curled down.

Her heart skipped a beat when she saw this, she didn't reply but lowered her eyes and continued walking. He cursed himself again for bringing the past up. Ok boy, he told himself, try again and do it right this time. He pointed to the various departments and blocks that they were passing and filled her in on the academic statistics. She nodded and kept the pretence up but her heart was feeling very heavy and her body – completely exhausted.

They arrived to a full house. Rhea and Aasma had returned, Paul was still there and so was Ryan who seemed equally at home with the girls. Her girls and the two boys were happily tucking into her cooking. She stopped at the door, basking in the life and warmth of the scene. She hadn't seen so much life in a room in a long time. Tears of joy were quickly wiped away along with the perspiration that the brisk walk had produced on her face and she entered the room beaming.

"Mom, we went to the circus. It was spectacular. It's so different over here, you know." Aasma was a bundle of excitement. "And Ryan won this teddy for me too."

"Mrs. Sud." Both the boys stood up when they saw her and Ryan extended his hand to greet her.

"Sorry we started without you mom, but we couldn't resist your cooking. Look at the boys, they love the daal, roti and chicken curry." Alia said feeding herself with a mouthful of the same.

"I'm so glad. I'll be happy to have you both over whenever you wish," she said very maternally. "Girls I have a surprise for you. I had gone to thank Dr Ahmed. He's come back here with me. He wanted to meet you Alia."

"Dr Ahmed, where is he?" Alia got up to greet him.

"Waiting by the door."

It was like a family reunion. Alia ran and hugged Aakash, Rhea and Aasma not wanting to be left behind did the same. Alia's kiss with death had brought them all together. Ryan and Paul each got a 'hey buddy' slap on the back. Amrita only stood watching his familiarity with her girls and how they loved him in return. Aasma had finally hugged her father, but only Amrita herself could bask in the knowledge. Aakash's 'one night of passion' had given him a daughter. *Look at her; don't you feel something special about her when you see her? Doesn't your body know she's a part of you when you hold her?* No, obviously not, she thought, if there was no space for her in his heart anymore, dear Aasma would not be able to get in edge wise. But then – he's a stranger, she reminded herself, not her Aakash.

They resumed lunch once again. Aakash was handed a plate by Aasma, "You have to eat with us Prof, my mom's a fantastic cook."

It was the first time that Aakash tasted her cooking and it was delicious. "Home made Indian food, Mrs. Sud, this is an absolute treat." He had kept his word. She thanked him politely.

She was glad that she had invested time in the kitchen and stocked the freezer. It took minutes to defrost some more food and see it disappear even faster into the eager mouths.

What a stupid man that husband of hers, Aakash thought. She was the perfect mother and a very gracious hostess, he knew her intellect and wit and he also knew how good she felt next to his body.

Lunch over, the boys excused themselves, happy to be

invited for a 'Biryani' dinner the coming Wednesday. It was Aasma's idea once again; "She's famous for her 'biryani'. You haven't eaten anything if you haven't eaten mom's biryani." she had said. Amrita was cornered into inviting them all. Aakash had tried to excuse himself but Aasma would hear none of it. "Oh please come Prof, if you don't come on Wednesday even I won't eat the brilliant, mouthwatering, scrumptious, aromatic ..."

"Stop girl stop, you'll have me salivating for the next three days. I'll be here and looking forward to meeting you all again, especially you, my little nymph." He tapped the tip of her nose with his fore finger as he said that.

Aasma had hugged him again, "Thanks Prof. I'll dress up just for you." She was laughing and so were the others on hearing that.

"Why thank you, I'm honoured young lady." He played along and bowed and Aasma complimented the act with a curtsy.

"Please bring Susan with you Professor, I'll call her up myself. I want to thank her too," Alia said.

"I will, thank you," he replied stealing a quick look at Amrita's reaction. She didn't show any. Susan had completely slipped out of his mind when he was with Amrita. He sprinted the rest of the way to the library, anything to help take Amrita out of his mind.

In the sanctity of her room Amrita opened her diary:

> For someone who had wanted a fresh start he remembers a lot of the past. No, he hasn't forgotten - and nor have I.
>
> Was that a dream or is this? Was that a reality or is this? Which is true - what my heart says or my mind? What a complicated web do we spin!

Lost Love's Labour

the unspoken word
the unsaid thought
the love between us
that came to naught

the unfulfilled dream
the unwritten song
the distance between
that's oh so long

the palpable vibrations
the unlived reality
the bond between us
that survived eternity.

CHAPTER 21

Her life was undergoing a sea change with too many things happening at the same time. She needed to sort her thoughts. The cool water of the pool felt good. She started her punishing routine of rapid continuous lengths, 'therapy' as she called it. Keep the mind blank, she ordered herself, but as fatigue set in she lost control over her command and her problems started unfolding themselves.

Almost losing Alia was probably the most traumatic experience of her life, more than even that evening she saw her parents fight. Thank God Alia came to consciousness, there was no saying what she would have done to avenge the loss. Professor Ahmed was right; when her latent nature surfaced she was no longer pretty. But she also realized that there were issues bigger than those one could fathom at a particular time. Perhaps if something worse than what had happened to Alia could happen, then that dreadful night her father fell never to rise again would be pushed to the third worst. Monumental events became irrelevant. Everything was relative - nothing constant.

To Aasma she owed Alia's second life. Even she, the cynic Rhea Sud, was moved by Aasma's grief. It was almost like Aasma, Alia and she had taken birth in their mother's womb at the same time; the bonding was so strong. Aasma had been trying to reach out to Alia but it seemed that at the same time she had reached out to Rhea too. She had awakened a chord of the original Rhea and brought some semblance of sanity in Rhea's life now. She was less angry at the world and a little more forgiving of her own self. She accepted Aasma into her life.

Her mother had arrived. No matter how many miles Rhea managed to put between them, her mother always caught up with her. What really got her goat was that Professor Ahmed was always doing that something extra for her mother. Why did he have to send her flowers thanking her for lunch, didn't the others have lunch too? Did they feel the need to do so? Why did he insist on doing the dishes with her while the rest of them teamed up for a game of dumb charades? Why did he look at her mother in that funny way when Susan was mentioned? Did he forget that she hated her mother? Whose friend was he anyway, her mother's? Wrong, he was her friend. So whose side should he be on? Maybe she would have to tell him her mother wasn't the angel she made herself out to be. He would then understand her grief and despise that woman too.

She started feeling dizzy; strange she thought to her self. She had never before felt dizzy in the water, exhausted yes. Time to leave perhaps; her 'therapy' was over anyway. The thoughts and emotions had sorted themselves and she now had a plan. All she had to do was wait for the perfect time to implement it.

CHAPTER 22

The days were short and the evenings got very cold. Her table was set, candles placed at both ends of it. Flowers took center stage on the table as well as the living room. She had brought in some potted ferns from the garden and placed them around the table lamps and re-arranged the furniture to give it an abstract, aesthetic appeal. Aakash and his fiancé were coming over and so she wanted everything to be perfect. Only building the fire, something she had never done in her life, was giving her a hard time. She'd managed to get it going, but by the time she took her shower and came back dressed for the evening, it was out. So she attacked it with new zeal one more time. She was nowhere near done when the doorbell rang. Dusting her trouser and adjusting her sweater she went to the door hoping the kids had come home from their movie.

She opened the door to find Aakash and his date, an attractive lady dressed in a maroon satin dress with a matching stole, shoes and bag. I should have worn my cashmere too Amrita mentally chided herself.

"Mrs. Sud," Aakash greeted her handing her a large bottle of Dom Perignon and a box of Sprungli chocolates, "for you."

"Thank you, you needn't have, really," she said a little embarrassed.

"Think nothing of it, please. Meet my fiancée, Susan. Susan this is Alia's and Rhea's mother." He introduced the two of them.

"Mrs. Sud, how delightful to finally make your acquaintance. Aakash has told me so much about you." She took Amrita's hand in hers and shook it politely.

"Well, he's certainly very possessive about you, he's kept you his big secret." She smiled back and welcomed them in. Actually in her mind she was amused at the way Susan pronounced his name.

Aakash kept a straight face but enjoyed this repartee between the two women. If only Amrita could hear herself, why even though it was a perfectly natural reply, she sounded almost jealous.

"I've had the time of my life trying to keep the fire going, I do apologize," she said trying to move a log of wood around.

"Allow me ma'am, we American's are better at this." Aakash took the log from her.

She moved away quickly, "Let me get the drinks then." She felt awkward with the two of them together in the room.

"Chill the champagne please, we'll open it later in the evening." Aakash requested her.

"Yeah, sure." The Chianti 1997 had been left to breathe and was perfect to the taste. As she poured them each a glass the doorbell rang once again, only this time it was a continuous clang. "Coming, coming," she said running to the door.

The girls, Ryan and Paul had all arrived together. No question of feeling awkward now. In fact she hardly needed to talk at all.

Thankful, she sat back and enjoyed the chatter around

her.

"Friends, we have reason to celebrate tonight." Aakash stood up to make a speech.

"Hear! hear!" The kids clapped and cheered him on.

"Thank you," he looked at Amrita and very politely said, "Mrs. Sud, that bottle of champagne…"

"I'll get it." Amrita went to get the bottle followed by Ryan and Paul who brought out whatever glasses they could find in the cabinet since the guesthouse wasn't equipped for a champagne party.

When each one had their glass, including Aasma who was served in a peg measure, Aakash continued.

"Friends we have reason to celebrate. Our dear Alia has been one brave girl."

"Ye-e-eah." All cheered on.

"She has also proved that she has immense strength and belief in love. She had gone very far away and it is love that brought her back. We are happy that she is well now and raise a toast to her health."

"To you Alia." Everyone chorused and drank up.

"There's more. I toast Rhea too. Her courage to stand up and fight an institution like figure gives me the conviction that here is a girl who will one day fight for a bigger truth and also lend her voice to those less strong. To you Rhea."

"To you Rhea." The chorus went again and took one more swig of the bubbly.

"Bear with me friends, my speech isn't over."

"Hear! hear!" They went again trying to take another sip.

"Wait you alcoholics. I call a toast to my little angel, Aasma. For were it not for her we may not have been celebrating at all."

"To you Aasma." They echoed happy to be sipping again.

"Now, last but not the least, I toast Mrs. Sud, the 'Mom', for bringing up these three wonderful sisters the way she has.

"To you Mom." The group were ready to empty their glasses.

"Wait," Amrita sat up. "I have a toast too." Tears had rolled out of her eyes, she let them; she didn't need to hide these from anyone.

"Professor Ahmed," she started, "Alia got a second life, I owe deep gratitude to you. Rhea did well; once again I stand to thank you. You have been a guardian angel to my family." She whispered the last few words almost choking with emotion, "I don't know what I would have done without you. Thank you so much."

The kids did for her what Aakash wanted to but could not. Ryan and Paul, both got up and went to her. Paul sat next to her, "Time for another hug, mom." He said as he hugged her tight.

Ryan offered her his handkerchief, which she accepted with an embarrassed laugh. He kissed her hand and took her glass for a refill,

"You need to get drunk Mrs. S."

Aasma came to her mother and sat on the floor with her back resting on Amrita's legs. Perfect, thought Aakash. Thank you God. It was up to him now to do something about her sombre mood.

"Well Mrs. S, there is one more reason that you could call a toast for me." All were attentive once again. "I received my doctorate results this evening and… I've passed."

Susan was the first to hug him, "Oh darling, congratulations, I am so proud of you," she said kissing him on the lips.

Aakash stole a quick look at Amrita who had turned her attention to her glass out of embarrassment.

"So what do we call you now?" Aasma wanted to know.

"Oh, you call him Doctor Ahmed dear," Susan replied for him.

"Doctor Ahmed. Hmm, the whole college will call you that Prof. I'll call you Doc…no, no, no, I'll call you Profdoc. Ok?" she asked him.

"Profdoc it shall be and you will be my little angel. OK?" He bowed and she returned the curtsy.

"Aren't you going to congratulate me, Mrs. Sud?" he said to her softly so only she could hear it. The others were busy with Susan; she was reciting famous toasts from various plays. He chose instead to indulge his heart, it was a special moment for him and he wanted her of all people to tell him she was proud as hell of his achievement.

"I'm sorry, you were mobbed over there by your fan club. You would not have heard me, so I decided to wait my turn. Congratulations Dr. Akaash Ahmed," she replied with a teasing smile.

He lifted his eyebrows in surprise, not expecting this spirited repartee from her, "The same old wicked Amrita." He said enjoying the intended dig at him.

"I'm sorry," she apologized, "I didn't mean to …"

"Love is never having to say you're sorry."

Her cheeks went red. Could he see through her charade?

"Even if there isn't any now, there was some of it a long time back, wasn't it?" he said. She didn't trust herself to open her mouth. He picked up his glass and made to leave, "I will always hear your voice Amrita, no matter how big the mob."

Rhea noticed all of Aakash's movements. Even though she was too far to hear the conversation she knew it was of a very personal nature. Their faces gave them away.

"Angel's famished mama," Little Aasma said rubbing her tummy.

"Everyone ready for dinner?" Amrita asked.

There was a unanimous roar that went 'Yeessss.'

"All on the table then, this is a special dish and you'll enjoy it more if you sit on the dining table and eat it with your hands, the Indian way. You know where the wash room is, cleaning your hands before you eat is another Indian habit." Amrita announced.

There was yet another unanimous roar that went 'Yeeessss mom.'

The candles were lit and an enormous serving bowl was brought out from the kitchen. "It's been sitting on the fire for hours and is very hot, be careful when you touch it." The vessel had been sealed with dough and Amrita made a big show of opening it and letting all at the table whet their appetite with the glorious aroma that escaped when she opened the bowl."

"Mmmm, smells divine," Said Paul.

"OK everybody, dig in." Once again Amrita sat back and enjoyed watching them all eat. How wonderful that Aakash could actually savour this specialty of hers. Never in her wildest dreams in the last ten years would she have believed that this could happen.

Out of the blue the electricity went off but the candles kept the room comfortably lit.

"That's the third time the generator's have tripped. It'll take 15-20 minutes for them to fix it," Aakash informed them, "but all the better for us, now we have a romantic dinner by candlelight. Right?"

"Tom Cruise isn't here, how can it be romantic?" Aasma piped in to everyone's amusement. "Let's tell ghost stories instead."

"Lets do that Angel, why don't you start?" Aakash suggested.

"Mom you ready?" Aasma asked Amrita.

"Ready." Amrita replied laughing, her hands covering her ears.

"What is this, Mrs. S, don't tell me ghost stories scare you?" Ryan asked her with equal pretence.

"Mom's a big sissy," Aasma told them all, "see I'll show you." Then she started enacting her story and Amrita played along. This was a game they had played ever since the twins would come home from school and tease her with one scary story after another, or at least what was meant to be scary.

Aasma started, "There was a daaark… daaark… house." She dragged her words and dropped its pitch.

At once Amrita's hands went to her ears and she gave her little girl the sweetest maternal smile ever and looking at her act Aasma broke into a laugh while narrating her lines. Aakash was having a very difficult time keeping his eyes off Amrita.

Aasma continued, "In the daaark… daaark… housssse there was a daaark... daaark…"

"I'll get the dessert." Amrita pretended she had a good excuse to run away.

"Sissy, sissy. . ." she heard them all chanting to her back.

Alone in the kitchen she stopped by the sink to catch her breath. The silver rays of the moon dancing with the moving clouds, kept the kitchen from total darkness. She stood there without lighting a candle. It was almost like she wanted to blend into the dark and become invisible. It was difficult to keep the act going and Aakash wasn't helping her any. She poured herself a glass of water and sipped it slowly waiting for her pulse rate to touch normal and the tears that were threatening her eyes again, to settle.

"Amrita." Aakash's deep seductive voice was disturbingly close.

"Huh?" she spun around surprised.

He was standing with a pile of soiled dishes in his hands. He looked at her for sometime before letting his face break into a smile, "If you're done with the sink I'll place these plates in them."

"Yes, of course." She took a step sideways and went towards the cabinets. She had to give an explanation for her melancholy so she said to him, "I was thinking of Aasma's father." No lie, she thought, as she tried to grope around for the matchbox.

She could not see his expressions, but her words had hit home hard, she could make that out by his body language. Aakash walked straight up to her, locked her in his arms and kissed her passionately. Then when he finally felt her responding to him he just as abruptly held her away and said, "You are a liar Mrs. Sud."

"How dare you," She said in a slow whisper filled

with emotion and rage. The lights came back on again. She certainly did not want him to see her flushed cheeks, so she turned her back to him and took a few steps forward. That was when, from the corner of her eye, she saw Rhea entering the kitchen. Amrita walked straight up to the oven as though that was her intention in the first place, pulled out a steaming apple pie from it and set it on the kitchen table. "Allow me," Aakash came up to her and said very formally.

"Why, thank you Dr. Ahmed." She took off the oven mittens and gave them to him. "I'll bring the ice-cream," she said going to the freezer.

The look on Rhea's face was hard to read but Aakash handled the situation well. "You were right Mrs. Sud, this is hot. Hey," he said like he'd just noticed Rhea, "you get the ice cream Rhea." He waited for her to take the ice cream from Amrita and then followed her out of the kitchen.

When the house was still and silence had voice again, Amrita reached for her diary. She clicked open her pen, delved into the most private chamber of her heart and started writing:

My body reacts with the same passion as it did then to his touch, to his kisses, to his words, his presence and even his thought. I had forgotten the powerful physical effect he has on me. Did I lose control or did I kiss him back in full control of my actions?

He could not have kissed me like that unless he felt the passion too. Passion, yes, it was clear now that lust and ego got the better of him. "You are a liar, Mrs. Sud." Did he do it to prove this fact to me? Whatever the lies and whoever the liar, there was but one truth. The truth he spoke of when he came and sat with me, 'I will always hear your voice Amrita, no matter how big the mob.'

He still cares.

COME SIT BY MY SIDE

Come sit by my side for
a while,
Steal a moment to not
to think.
Tomorrow will bring
more lies,
Let me drown in the
depth of your eyes.

I've loved you when
you loved me,
I still did when you
denied.
When I look at life in
my heart's mirror,
You're a part of me I
can't hide.

Smile - and the memory will engrave upon my soul,
Synonymous with my name is your story - untold.
Each tear that I don't cry
Burns within my being,
Bearing witness to my love and…
…and my unfulfilled dream.

Come sit by my side for a while,
Steal a moment to not to think.
Tomorrow will bring more lies,
Let me drown in the depths of your eyes.

CHAPTER 23

Alia was very nervous. She had never visited a criminal court before, even if this was a specially convened court for this case. Never in her life dreamt that her word would decide the course of justice. Her mother, Rhea, Aasma, Dr. Ahmed, Ryan and Paul had all come to give moral support. They were escorted to their seats and were waiting for the judge to arrive.

She still could not believe the story that the Dean had told her. It seemed unbelievable to him too, Mr. Francis had said.

When the police had arrived Bobwana was sitting beside Ulfat. Ulfat had been stabbed in the stomach and had already bled to death. The murder weapon, a metal picket fence, the same as that found in the boys hostel, was thrown to one side. Bobwana was covered with blood. The police had arrested her on charge of murder in the first degree and Ulfat's body was sent for post mortem.

Everyone who knew her wanted to believe that Bobwana was innocent. The police decided to keep her in custody till they solved the crime. They could not let her come back to the hostel for her own safety and that of the other students too. Forty-eight hours later the post mortem results came as a shock. Ulfat was pregnant. It was an early pregnancy. DNA testing and interrogations led the trail straight to Irfan. Irfan and Bobwana were then questioned afresh and simultaneously in adjacent rooms. That was when the sequence of events became clear.

Ulfat came from a very strict Muslim home. She had never spoken to boys to whom she was not related. Her grades were so good that her father was persuaded to allow her to come to the US to further her education. Living in a sexually liberated society now and being deprived herself she indulged in a lesbian relationship with Bobwana. For Bobwana it was more than a casual relationship, she had had too many of them with too many boys. This was the first time Bobwana realized that she was a lesbian and was actually in love with Ulfat. When Ulfat fell in love with Irfan she tried to talk her out of it knowing the kind of boy that he was. Ulfat would hear nothing of it and so Bobwana left her alone.

Irfan was an arrogant boy. He thought he could sleep with any girl he wanted. Ulfat would not comply no matter how hard he tried. Marriage was the all-important prerequisite for her before sex. What did he care, if marriage was what she wanted, so be it. He bribed three of his friends to sign on a false marriage certificate and stand witness as he recited the sacred words 'Nikah', three times. He convinced her that they should keep this their big secret till they could both visit her parents during the next summer break and only then would they announce it officially. He knew Ulfat was crazy about him, so he played his ace and gave her an ultimatum - that she marries him now or else never. That he had agreed to marry her because he loved her. If she stalled it, then perhaps he might change his mind. She was happy to marry him at last, he was happy to bed her at will. This marriage of convenience lasted only a short while though, for Ulfat found out that she was pregnant. When she gave Irfan the news, he was livid. He claimed he had nothing to do with her and walked out.

The night Alia found her missing, she had decided to

go to the boy's dormitory and make him see reason one last time. She called him on his roommate's cellphone and told him to meet her near the tennis courts. If he didn't come she would go straight to the Dean and tell him how he duped her into marriage.

Irfan had to comply for she was becoming a nuisance. He told her to go wait at the tennis courts and he would arrive soon. When he did arrive he was carrying a metal picket fence with him. He hid it in the bush. He would first hear her out and then tell her what to do. If she was a good girl she would live, if not…he would have to come back for it. He certainly did not want a stupid pregnant girl ruining his life.

Bobwana was headed to the boy's dorm when she heard muffled cries and angry voices coming from the tennis courts. She followed the sounds and stopped short behind a bush when she realized it was Ulfat and Irfan.

Her parents would first kill her and then themselves too if they found this out, she heard Ulfat tell Irfan. They were married, so what was so wrong with having the baby? In his rage Irfan told her about how he had deceived her because she was a prude. He didn't love her. He showed her the marriage certificate and laughed as he tore it to and threw it at her face. 'You were a useless lay anyway, who wants to get stuck to you for life?' He had said to her. She was shattered and furious and threatened to go to the Dean right that minute. 'Oh no you don't,' he'd said, 'I didn't want to do this but you leave me no choice. Say good-bye to the world you bitch.' With that he came to pick up his weapon. But Bobwana was quicker than him when she saw what he was after, "No!" she had said snatching the metal rod and charging at him with it. He in turn ran towards Ulfat and threw her onto the sharp point of the metal.

Ulfat just slumped on to Bobwana's shoulder and

then onto the ground. Bobwana stood there looking at her bleeding friend in complete shock. She heard Irfan's voice as he started running back, 'You did that, you did that to Ulfat'. She remembered her own rage when she saw him try to run away after what he had done and gave chase, still tightly clasping the metal rod. He was too fast for her and when she saw the closed doors of the dorm she realized he had escaped. That was when she remembered Ulfat and ran back to help her. But she was too late. She knew by the deathly stillness of her open eyes that Ulfat was dead. In complete shock herself she just sat beside Ulfat's body till a security personnel found them.

Irfan was in custody too ever since that confession. Both he and Bobwana would appear before court in two days. It was mandatory that Alia come to court since she was a major witness in the case. Whether she was psychologically ready for the trial or not, her friend needed her.

The courtroom was packed with people. The Dean and other faculty members, the security personnel, students and the press, they were all there already. It was easy to identify the families of Bobwana and Irfan. Both were seated in the front row too but to her right. Ulfat's family was seated behind them. She could not bear to face them for fear that she would break down. She could not bring herself to look at the families of Bobwana or Irfan either; it felt as though they were begging her for mercy. So she just looked ahead. Aakash and Rhea were sitting on either side of her. Rhea took Alia's hand in hers and gently squeezed it, "You'll do well, I know it. I'm with you. Don't be scared."

"Thanks." Alia was on the verge of tears already.

Aakash had briefed her and had described the courtroom to her in detail before they had arrived. He practiced cross-examining her like the prosecutors would so that they would not intimidate her. Time had been short and Alia was still not ready but there was nothing they could do about it.

The large door in front opened and Bobwana and Irfan were escorted in. Alia let out a gasp when she saw them hand cuffed and started sobbing softly.

"Hold yourself together Alia. Don't lose it. You owe this to your dead friend," Aakash admonished, intentionally choosing hard words to bring home the truth.

"Yes sir," She said accepting his handkerchief gaining control of her self again.

"All rise," the footboy ordered.

They all stood up as the judge entered. The court was brought to order and the case presented to him. One by one the prosecuting and defending lawyers would summon various witnesses to testify, question them and then send them back. Finally Alia was called upon the witness stand. She froze in her seat unable to move.

"Alia, they're calling you," Rhea tried.

"Not a big deal Alia, look back at Ulfat's mother. Look back Alia. You've gone through worse and come victorious, you can do this. Just look at Ulfat's mother and tell me you don't see the face of your own mother in her, begging you to bring to justice her daughter's killer. Turn around Alia." Aakash ordered her firmly and she did. Ulfat's mother was crying silently and when Alia turned around to look at her she brought her hands in front of her like a prayer waiting to be answered.

That was all it took. Alia knew what she had to do and without a word but a silent promise to Ulfat's mother she took her place in the witness stand. It didn't matter what they asked and what tricks they tried; she was firm in her replies.

"Are you sure Ms. Sud? It is possible that your friend was caught in a love triangle and so out of sheer jealousy and scorn she killed Ulfat then framed Mr. Irfan Khureshi? Killing two birds with one stone literally. Is it not possible?"

"Objection!"

The lawyer defending Irfan was getting nasty.

"Or maybe Ms. Sud, Ms. Bobwana, who claims to be too much in love with Ulfat to want to kill her, has a lesbian affair going on with you too and you are trying to protect her."

"Objection!"

Alia's face went white, what was this man insinuating in front of so many people?

But he wasn't done. "Or maybe," he came very close to her and with one hand leaning on the wooden railing he said to her with a wicked smile, "maybe the two of you planned this murder together because it is possible that Ms. Ulfat found out about you and was going to squeal on you? Yes? Or is Bobwana in this alone and you have no idea about what she was up to?"

"Objection! Your Honour."

Alia's shock was apparent for all to see. Each and every one in the courtroom was stunned too. But of all of them it was she who was fastest to recover, even faster than the prosecuting attorney who stood up to object.

She held her hand out asking him to sit then started her reply in the same tone as that nasty lawyer.

"Perhaps, Your Honour, it was our honourable defending attorney who maybe wanted fame and so could possibly have lured my unsuspecting friends to the tennis courts and then maybe drugged all of them and done the needful or perhaps hired cronies to do the dirty work or maybe…"

"Order, order." The judge slammed his hammer down to silence the hysterical performance. "You will stand in contempt of court, young girl, unless you are able to explain your outburst."

"Your Honour, I know what he was trying to do. With all the 'maybes and perhaps' his fabricated story was only trying to unnerve me so that I would wash my hands clean off Bobwana and then he could have a field day implicating her. He's good, Your Honour," she said looking at Irfan's lawyer, "but he forgets that truth has a strength of its own."

The courtroom resonated with a thunder of applause. Aakash had held his breath and now let it out in relief. She'll do just fine, his Alia, he thought.

"Bobwana was fast asleep that night. I had to wake her up. She was a true friend of Ulfat's, more than I was anyway. She was ready to brave the consequences of being caught outside the dorm that late at night. I was not." Alia started crying but did not stop. "I was happy waiting for Ulfat to come back. Then I was waiting for them both to come back. But I didn't leave the dorm till it was permissible. You think she could have committed this ghastly act? Never. Ask that boy you are defending, ask him why he ran away if he was innocent? Ask him why he didn't help the woman who was carrying his child? Ask him what he said to me when I refused to sleep with him. I'll save you another lie Irfan, I'll tell them what you said and I have the entire French class to back me up.

'You'll sleep with me woman. Willingly or unwillingly you'll spread your legs for me.'

Amrita stifled a sob with her hands. Dear God, what

hell had she subjected her daughters to?

Alia wiped her tears and continued, "It was Bobwana again who cared enough to stand up for me. Ever since then I have lived in fear of being raped by Irfan and his friends. Ask that boy you are defending to give you every gory detail of my friend's murder. He'll give it to you first hand, won't you Irfan?" she looked him in the eye with such rage as would have burned a hole through a mountain. He met her eyes and then looked down. "Bobwana is a friend's truest friend. I am lucky and proud to be a friend of hers. I trust her with my life more than I trust myself. Bobwana is definitely innocent, Your Honour." Alia sat back drained of every ounce of energy.

"We'll let the jury decide that. Has the defence had enough or is there any more?" the judge asked.

"The defence rests, Your Honour."

"Thank you Ms. Sud. That was indeed very brave of you. But next time don't mess with the court," the judge advised her.

"I pray there never is a next time, Your Honour."

"Amen to that."

There was nothing more to be said or heard so the court adjourned for a three day recess over the long weekend.

CHAPTER 24

The judge had ordered three days recess. That was a long time to wait doing nothing, especially now, that Alia was feeling much better. It was a long weekend, since Foundation Day, a day when the entire college got the day off, fell on Monday.

All three girls left for a three-day skiing vacation with Ryan and Paul. Amrita had no intentions of being a spoke in the wheel and managed to convince them that she was looking forward to the rest and she would perhaps meet her friend Monica too. The girls weren't too excited about that but they kept their prejudice to themselves.

She had called Monica on the phone the very next morning and was glad that she was free to meet her immediately. Monica came to fetch her in a smart looking car. 'Wow' Amrita had thought mentally.

"Amrita, how wonderful it is to finally meet you. You look good."

Monica greeted her from the car and indicated with the wave of her hand that she should come and sit in it too.

"Hello Monica, I've been looking forward to meeting you too." Amrita got into the passenger seat and stretched out to hug her school friend.

Monica put the car into drive and took off at quite a speed. "I'm sorry I didn't meet you earlier. I was unwell and ..."

"I know and I understand, don't worry," Amrita

reassured her.

"You know? What do you know?"

"I know, you were admitted into a clinic for treatment."

"How do you know that?" Monica asked, surprised.

"Well, when Aasma, my youngest daughter was arriving here, you were to fetch her from the airport. The girls got a call telling them all this and so they made other arrangements." Amrita had an uneasy feeling that all was still quite not so well with Monica, so she refrained from giving out any details about all that had happened with them in the last few weeks.

"May I ask what you were being treated for?"

"On inconvenient pregnancy."

"Oh!" Amrita exclaimed sympathetically trying her hardest not to let Monica guess that she wanted to know more.

"Yes, I remember now that I was to collect Aasma. But who called you if it wasn't me?" Monica asked.

"Secretary to a Mr. Brian Coplan." Amrita remembered the girls discussing him.

"Oh, I see." Monica stepped on the accelerator.

Amrita was getting nervous; maybe this wasn't a very good idea. The girls had been right in their reading of her, Monica was a messed up woman.

It wasn't long before they heard the siren of the cop car. Monica pulled over to side and was given a ticket for speeding.

"Damn," she cursed.

"Let's go to that park Monica, it'll be easier to talk." Amrita suggested.

"Yes, let's do that."

They selected a corner bench and sipped their coffees.

"What's with you Monica and who is Brian Coplan?" Amrita asked feigning ignorance even though Alai had told her a lot already.

"Brian is an extremely successful businessman and he and I are going steady." Monica wanted to make sure that Amrita knew he was very rich but she wanted to be brief on this subject. Brian's change of heart had sent her into a clinic once already and she wasn't quite sure where she stood with him at that moment.

"But he is a married man Monica," said Amrita.

"So what? He's unhappy with his wife and he'll leave her and come to me." Monica justified.

"He's unhappy with his wife? Monica, all marriages go through troubled waters; your presence only complicates matters for them, can't you see that?" Amrita asked.

"His marriage is not working out, I am the one he loves, so what's wrong with that?" Monica was adamant.

"Everything, Monica, it makes you his mistress. If you are happy with that then there's nothing more to be said."

"I will not stay his mistress for long, he will divorce his wife and marry me." Monica said confidently.

"Is that what he says or you?" Amrita questioned her.

"I have worked hard and long on winning his love, I will be Mrs. Brian Coplan."

"Winning his love? My goodness! The girls were right about you; you are one conniving, selfish woman. What is it that you are trying to win, his love or money power and a new lifestyle for yourself? Is that car a payoff for sleeping with him too?"

"Amrita!" Monica said threateningly.

"Don't Amrita me. You are no different from Gayatri. Do you know who she was? She was you Monica; she was the woman who destroyed my life. She wanted to marry my husband too, God alone knows what good sense prevailed on Rahul and he left her and came back to us."

"Stop it Amrita." Monica was furious but Amrita was unstoppable.

She got up to leave, then leaning over she warned, "Brian will do the same Monica, one day he'll see through you and appreciate what he had. And Monica even if you manage to rope him into marriage you will have to live with guilt, for in the eyes of everyone you will always remain what you are now – a whore! Live with that."

Monica raised her hand to slap Amrita, but Amrita caught it in time.

"Never underestimate the wrath of a woman scorned, Monica. If nothing, then her pain will be the noose around your neck."

Amrita threw Monica's hand aside in disgust and walked away.

CHAPTER 25

As soon as Monica was out of sight Amrita broke into a run. She chose a beaten track that went straight into the woods. Anyplace where she could lose herself and avoid human contact was where she wanted to be. The tall avenue of pine trees, the flora and fauna - all became a mass of blur that were passing her by as she fought back her tears. She had not cried in a long time and was definitely not going to let a no-good like Monica break her. Life had thrown harsh challenges at her and she had learnt to cope with the unexpected. Meeting Monica was something else though. She had looked forward to spending a relaxed morning with her schoolmate, a friend she had trusted her girls with. What she got was a face-to-face confrontation with her nightmare. She had met Gayatri. Perhaps a much more clever Gayatri. A conniving and therefore more evil and dangerous Gayatri.

She ran until her lungs screamed, then slowed to a jog when she saw an opening in the woods. Ahead of the clearing was a natural pond big enough to house a family of swans. Thick woods framed its outer circumference. Panting, Amrita sat at a comfortable distance from the waters edge. The swans drifting around in a close cluster was a very soothing sight.

It had been a long time since she had lost control of her emotions but strangely she now felt relief instead of anger. Gayatri had become the bane of her existence but Amrita had been too weak and helpless against Rahul to do anything about it. The twins were her weakness and Rahul knew it and used it to make her do his bidding. She had done so but how many times had she dreamt of walking up to Gayatri in public and telling her off? How many times had she stopped herself from wishing Gayatri were dead? How many nightmares had that woman given her and she had awoken to find her life a living hell?

Meeting Monica actually made her realize how lucky she herself was that it was Gayatri and not Monica that had come into her life. Gayatri, the social opportunist, a promiscuous status seeker, who used her body and charm as bait. Unlike Monica, who used her body, charm and a lethal weapon that Gayatri did not posses – her intellect.

In telling Monica off she realized how deeply she felt about family values. Yes, she had fallen in love with Aakash, but it wasn't with purpose and intention and certainly was not a part of a master plan. There was a world of difference between the Monicas and Gayatris and her. It wasn't a question of righteousness but rightness. It wasn't about having double standards but taking a stand. Gayatri's shadow had loomed large in her life but now that she had faced it she had finally broken free of the shackles of guilt. It wasn't she who was at fault - but Gayatri and Rahul! Guilty as charged! She could now live life not only for her girls but for herself too.

Smiling to herself she feasted her eyes once again on the family of swans that had now drifted to the far end of the pond. She looked deep into the woods ahead and could only visualize the law of the jungle apply: survival of the fittest. In the human world 'fittest' would have to mean physical, mental, psychological, emotional and spiritual soundness collectively. Without a strong value system there would be no premise to work these upon. She had survived. The woods stood tall and proud and so did she,

she realized, as she rose and dusted the dried leaves off the seat of her jeans. Retracing her steps through the woods and walking back to the main gate of the park, she was now able to absorb and enjoy the aesthetics of the forest, the aroma of the woods and the harmonious chirping of the birds. She hailed a taxi back to the college campus.

CHAPTER 26

"Hello."

"Hi."

"Aakash?"

"Tom Cruise."

"You wish."

"Lovely day."

"Yes."

"Let's enjoy it."

"Pardon?"

"You have plans for today?"

"Um…"

"Good, I'm coming to fetch you."

"But, the girls are away skiing."

"I know."

"They'll be back the day after tomorrow."

"I know."

"Founder's Day, your day off too?"

"Yes."

"You mean Susan, you and I?"

"No."

"Susan and I?"

"Yes."

"What?"

"You deserved that."

"I did."

"So?"

"I don't know."

"Why? Don't trust me?"

"Don't trust myself."

"I'm counting on that."

"Excuse me?"

"No testing Mrs. Sud, I promise."

"I'm counting on that."

"Come on. Just look out of your window."

"It's lovely."

"It is."

"How soon can you fetch me?"

"Ten minutes."

"Don't be late."

He smiled at her favourite line.

"Where are we going?"

"Does it matter?" He saw her hesitate, "I mean we're in this dream car, the day is clear and sun shines happily, the trees, flowers, birds – they all bask in the freedom of spring; so why can't we?"

"Freedom." She pronounced the word as though she had just been presented with it.

"Free to be you, free to laugh, love and live, to cry, to sing or dance or just sit with your thoughts and enjoy the drive," he added. "Music, yes, we need music." He reached for the remote and selected a CD.

Soon the soothing strains of the saxophone replaced all thoughts in her head and with a sigh she settled deeper into the cushioned seats of the convertible Jaguar and let her senses drink deep into the glory of nature.

The drive was indeed very pretty, specially once they had left the city limits. Open green pastures and a clear blue sky and nothing else to cloud the mind, this was pure bliss. The car was travelling at the speed of sound or at least it seemed so and it felt like with every second she was able to put a huge amount of physical distance between herself and her responsibilities. Freedom, it was exhilarating. But what was completely unbelievable was the fact that Aakash was here with her, driving her through her dream.

She turned to look at him.
He turned to look at her too.
She smiled and so did he.

'*If only*...' she thought.
'*If only*...' he thought.
I wish I could hold your hand and drive.
I wish I could hold your hand while you drove.
Thank you Amrita for accepting, you made my life.
Thank you Aakash for inviting me, you made mine.

They drove a long distance just happy to be together, the cold February wind and the warm sun making a heady combination.

"Coffee?" he asked her.
"Only if you want some."

"Let's just."

She smiled and nodded her response. "OK."

He pulled over at a café's drive in window and collected two cappuccinos and a large choco-chip cookie.

"This is the life," he said to her as he sipped the hot liquid, "The sexy saxophone playing beneath the open skies, a hot coffee, a gooey cookie and thou beside me sitting in my sports convertible and the world is paradise enow."

She giggled.

"See, I too can do poetry, even if it's misquoting at its worst."

"The modern day Rubaiyat," she laughed.

He laughed too.

"You are still so beautiful," he told her.

She blushed and replied, "You look good too."

"Only good?"

"Huh?"

"Not great?"

"Great," she endorsed.

"Not gorgeous great?"

She looked at his wicked expression and smiled with a naughty look in her eyes too.

"Not to die for handsome?"

She started laughing.

"Not …"

"Stop it." She said, laughing still, "Tom Cruise is Tom Cruise. Accept it."

"There goes my Hollywood dream."

"May I ask you a personal question?" she asked him after a while.

He took his time, as though contemplating her request. "No, I'm not a virgin," he said with a straight face.

She burst out laughing and couldn't stop. He loved to see her relaxed and having a good time. She took her role as 'mom' too seriously. Perhaps she had to. There was just too much on her plate. But for these few hours he would give her as much happiness as he could.

"Oh, you mean it wasn't that? In that case you may ask me anything."

"Where is Susan? She's your fiancée, wouldn't she object to this?"

"Susan?"

"Yes."

"Do you remember Jaan…I mean Amrita, sorry about that," he said hitting himself at the back of his head, "Do you remember me telling you how most of us get married for all the wrong reasons?"

"Uhuh."

"I almost did the same thing, can you believe that? I realized that I wasn't being fair to her or myself. Fortunately I saw the light of day in time and last night we called off our engagement."

He saw the disbelief on her face. "Mona Lisa, that's you. I don't know whether you're happy or sad."

Amrita had felt a sense of elation that she tried to hide at once. "She's a lovely girl."

"She is, and I am a very eligible bachelor again."

"You are…" She said then added after a short pause, " unsettled once again."

"Really?"

"Yup."

He thought for a while, "It's the breeze," he said very seriously.

"What's the breeze?"

"This unsettled look." He ran his fingers through his hair.

"Normally I'm very settled."

She burst out laughing again and slapped him gently on his arm.

"Aakash, you haven't changed. And don't give me a wise crack on that now."

"You haven't changed either, Lady Hitler."

"You remember a lot."

"Don't you?"

She had to change the subject. "So this a celebration of freedom for me and you."

"Absolutely right, my lady." he replied. "And we shall celebrate in style. First we'll visit The Loray Caverns. They are famous for their natural formation of stalactites and stalagmites. These things have even been used as natural tuning forks and a computerized system produces a melody through them. You'll love it."

"Wow, that's wonderful. Thank you. And then?" she asked eagerly.

"And then we'll go skinny dipping in the natural clear water pool as per custom," he said quickly and very matter-of-factly.

"What?"

It was his turn to laugh heartily. She realized he was

only kidding and slapped his arm again in mock anger. "Horrible man."

'What?' He imitated her and she laughed even more.

'What?' he exaggerated her expression while imitating her again.

She was hysterical with laughter. She laughed till tears rolled out of her eyes. He was laughing with her too.

Then the most unexpected thing happened. The tears of joy turned to tears of grief, tears of years and years of pent up grief. She started sobbing uncontrollably. Aakash immediately pulled over at the first available opportunity.

He drew himself closer to her and whispered her name, "Amrita."

She turned and went straight into his arms crying uncontrollably into his shoulder, her body almost convulsing as the barrage of tears broke lose.

He held her close to him, as close as he could to his heart.

"I'm sorry Aakash, I'm so sorry. Oh God…I didn't mean this to happen… I thought I couldn't cry anymore… lived through it all…made myself numb…but…but…"

"It's ok Jaan, it's ok. You've been very brave. It's only going to get better. All that is behind you."

"I… I…oh Aakash." She clung to him.

When her tears finally stopped he pulled her face up to his. It was streaked with tears and smudged make up; she couldn't have looked prettier to him. "I had promised not to test Mrs Sud, but I made no promises about kissing Amrita."

He waited for her response. She looked into his eyes

and slowly reached her lips up to his; barely touching them she waited there feeling his warm breath on her face. Then moving her arm around his neck she pulled him deep into her mouth.

When finally they drew apart there was no pretense left between the two. Their passion for each other was apparent to both. Her eyes had that familiar glazed look and every cell in his body was longing to burst within her. Yet, he dare not take liberties and spoil it again for both of them.

"Hello Amrita." He smiled at her stroking her cheek.

"Hello Aakash." She understood at once.

"Long time."

"Too long."

"Where have you been?"

She pointed to his heart questioningly.

"Nope, I checked several times, you'd checked out." He teased and kissed her again.

She took her eyes off his face and snuggled into his chest instead.

"Feeling better?" he asked her.

She shook her head in the negative. "Nope."

He smiled at her lie. Sighed and held her close to him again. His fingers played with her hair. He wished he could freeze time, but moving on was inevitable. They were after all on a highway.

"You want to change places Jaan?" he said softly into

her hair.

"Huh?"

"Would you mind balancing on this pointed gear lever while I snuggle against those." He eyed her breasts.

Embarrassed but once again tickled to the bone by his humour she drew away from him.

"To the caves, James."

"Yes ma'am."

He took her hand in his, kissed it and held it as he drove to the grotto.

The caves had been as wonderful as he had described them to be. It was sheer beauty inside the mouth of the earth. Walking the natural and man made tracks; they explored the different levels of the cavern and admired the awesome stalactite formations. Being together gave an absolutely new dimension to the aesthetics of the caves. Later they went on a long exploratory walk of the area.

The Blue Ridge Mountains provided a perfect canvas for the setting sun. A riot of colours in hues of orange and red had spread themselves around the mountain peaks. It seemed as if the sun had done its days work and was now happy to melt into and rest in the strong and welcoming arms of the mountains.

He guided her towards a tavern with a quaint looking Italian restaurant. "This way, my lady."

The Maître de took them to a table for two that had been previously reserved. Candles were lit and a chilled bottle of Californian wine was poured into their bohemian stem glasses but only after Aakash had approved of it. A quartet stood around them strumming their instruments and singing popular, old romantic songs.

"You sure know how to do it in style." She said, high on the heady feeling of being with Aakash without any pretences. Freedom, if only for a day, would be theirs.

"You ain't seen nothing babe." He winked at her.

She blushed.

He reached out and clasped her hands in his. "I wanted you to feel special," he said to her.

"I do," she said. "But how can I make you feel special?" she asked and regretted it almost instantly when she saw him laughing.

"That's the perfect toast. Let's drink to us." He lifted his glass to hers.

"To us," she said and took a couple of quick thirsty sips.

"Amrita and Aakash." He toasted and almost finished his glass.

"To destiny, that has woven our lives together," she added.

"To destiny that brings us together despite ourselves. To togetherness." He emptied his glass with that.

The musicians had positioned themselves on the podium and continued to play. Hot spaghetti and homemade bread with olive oil and chili made a sumptuous meal.

"What a beautiful evening! Was that a falling star or am I seeing things?" she giggled feeling the wine go to her head.

"Let's take our glasses to the deck, there's a clear view of the sky from there," he suggested.

The view was indeed breathtaking. On a clear night like

this a million stars were visible, blinking in tandem to some silent astral melody. The moon was less than half a crescent. It was cold and Amrita drank large sips of wine to keep warm.

"Heaven on earth." She sighed wishing her life to be so tranquil ever more. "It must be freezing up at the ski resort."

He nodded leaning against the parapet and sipping his wine but with his gaze fixed on her.

There was something about the girls that was disturbing her; she decided to bring it up with him. For once she would not be alone in decision-making. "The twins have steady boyfriends already." She quietly observed.

He kept silent; she had more on her mind he knew.

"The girls have grown. The world has changed too. I wonder,…" She looked into her glass again.

She could not bring her self to say it.

"Doesn't matter, let it be." She tried to dismiss her discomfort.

He put down his wine glass on the ledge and then did the same with hers while pulling her into his arms.

"It matters, but there's precious little one can do about it. They are both adults now and they've both got a good head on their shoulders. The good thing is that both Ryan and Paul are very decent boys. How serious the commitment or far they want to take it - now that is something they will decide for themselves. If its sex that's worrying you then yes, this is a free society. But then it is the same anywhere in the world today. You have to believe that your girls know what they are doing. They have a lot of character, both Alia and Rhea. I trust them with their lives."

She looked tentative despite his assurance. " I hope they don't have regrets."

"I hope so too. But hey, we all make our share of mistakes, don't we?"

She nodded her agreement.

"Then let them make theirs. Just pray the mistakes aren't too painful and be there to hug them if they come to you for one." He ran a finger along her cheek. "Makes sense?"

"Always makes sense when it comes from you," she replied now feeling more at ease mentally. "What a great father you would make."

He pulled her closer to him. "Actually there's something else I'm better at, but we'll leave that for now." She went pink in the cheeks.

"You remember Jaan, when we had met in Jammu you had said that for one day you just wanted you to be you – Amrita. Not mom, wife or anything else?"

"Yes."

"Tonight I revel in holding the complete Amrita next to me. The mother," he kissed her forehead. "The business woman," he kissed her eyes. "The wife, another man's wife, but I'm going to kiss you anyway," she smiled and he kissed her nose. "Last but not the least, I revel in holding Amrita, 'the person' as you call it. I can't believe I have you here with me like this. Don't wake me from this dream Jaan."

She recited the verse from her diary:

Hold me in your arms for a while,
Steal some moments to not to think,
Tomorrow will bring more lies,
Let me drown in the depths of your eyes

She smiled at him shyly when she finished.

"And let me melt in the magic of your smile." He replied and retrieved the wine glasses, "To stolen moments," he toasted.

"To stolen moments," she reiterated and drank the glass through.

He laughed and did the same.

The evening had matured and with it slowed the tempo of the music. Aakash heard the soothing strains of 'Strangers in The Night' coming through the lounge.

Taking the empty glass from her he asked her, "Dance with me?"

"Love to."

Locked in each other's arms and oblivious to the world they moved in blissful unison. "I like it…" she spoke into his neck. "I like it when you call me 'Jaan'," she said bashfully.

He laughed silently and pulled his head away to look at her again. "Jaan," he said with all the passion in him, "Jaan, Jaan, Jaan." And then brought his lips down on hers.

His kiss had a wild urgency right from the start. Aakash pulled Amrita even closer to him. His hands were longing to explore every curve of her body. He slid his hands under her shirt and felt the bare, warm smoothness of her waist while his tongue explored her sweet wet mouth.

She felt her urgency keeping pace with his. The last time that she had made love to a man was to him. It was like everything else that had happened to her body between then and now did not matter.

She kissed him back with equal lust and love and felt a surge of liquid between her legs when his hands touched her skin. Her breathing became rapid as his hands climbed up towards her breasts. She then felt his hesitation as he stopped just short of her bra line. She withdrew her mouth from his and looked at him, "Don't stop, Aakash."

She had given her consent. Holding her close to him and looking straight into her beautiful face, his eyes locked with hers, he moved his hands up over her bra to cup her breast in his palm and then pressed into it till she reacted.

"Oh God, Aakash," she said leaning her body against him, unable to support herself against the tide of passion that claimed dominance over her mind and body.

"Not here," he said huskily slipping his hands out and taking a few deep breaths. "Let's get out of here."

He cleared the bill and then holding her hand he led her to the reception.

CHAPTER 27

The room was small and dark when they entered it. An electric fire switched itself on when the electronic key was slipped into its holder, giving the room a warm glow and ample subdued light.

As soon as the door shut behind them Aakash pressed Amrita against the wall of the narrow foyer with his body. Using one hand on the wall for support he held Amrita's face with the other as they kissed slow and deep. Whilst their lips were busy claiming each other Aakash explored her body relishing every curve and fullness, wanting to rediscover and savour the familiar feel of her body. He slipped his hand under her shirt and traced her trouser line, then let out a muffled groan when his thumb found her belly button. Travelling down her waist, he moved to the low of her back pulling her close to him and pressing himself into her at the same time. Amrita was almost delirious with excitement. She unbuttoned his shirt and pushed it aside, driving him completely insane with her mouth and fingers. He let her do what she wanted; completely paralyzed by the amazing sensations she was creating in his body. Her mouth was electrifying against his skin and was creating waves of pleasure in him.

When he could contain it no more he lifted her mouth to his and let their lips meet, savouring the softness of what had just driven him completely insane. As their lips interlocked for a seemingly unending eternity, his tongue explored the innermost softness of her mouth reaching for its counterpart in hers. Slowly he pushed her shirt up moving back slightly to allow him to slip it off her and expose a body that looked simply divine. A white underwired bra gave her breasts an exquisite fullness above the lace and her flat stomach met her trousers with the gentle and smooth curve of her waist. She was the most beautiful woman he had ever seen.

"Oh God! Amrita. How I've missed you." He groaned as he touched the smooth skin of her breasts and kissed it before bringing his mouth over the lace and biting her through it. She gasped for breath with the sudden and unexpected pain and pleasure and her hand instinctively drew him closer into her. Amrita smiled when Aakash guided her hand to show her how desperately he desired her. He undid her trousers and let it fall around her feet. She stepped out supporting herself against him. He then reached up and removed her hairclip and her hair fell cascading around her shoulders and back. The picture was perfect.

"Come to me, my pretty." He said to her as he scooped her in his arms and carried her into the room and gently laid her on the bed.

She took her time admiring his body as he undid his cufflinks walking to the French windows and out onto the large patio to check it for privacy. It was secure.

"Let's make this special, Jaan," he said to her as he stepped back into the room removing his shirt. With that he wrapped her in the comforter she was lying on and scooped her into his arms again and then lay her down on the wooden floor of the patio.

The sky looked breathtaking, a panoramic view of the entire solar system it seemed. The air held the delicate fragrance of pine. The occasional sounds were only those from a world very distant from theirs. Taking his time undressing her, kissing and whispering endearments he went into her sweetness drinking, sucking and teasing her to a wild abandon. Her body was writhing with pleasure and her moans drove him to a frenzy of excitement. The sensations that he was creating were taking her to increasing levels of ecstasy. She too brought him to a plane that was way above the norm. Sensations floated by as their desires demanded fulfillment. He deftly freed himself off his clothes and then gently pressed himself against her.

"I have no protection, Jaan," he said to her.

"I want to feel you in me Aakash, I want to feel you inside me. I'm safe."

"So am I. Trust?"

Surrendering to the all-consuming passion of her innermost core she looked at him and smiled, "Dr Ahmed, I'm going to rape you if you tease me any more."

He smiled back and holding captive her glazed and passionate eyes with his, he gently eased himself into her and then with a final deep thrust he entered her completely.

She gasped, arching her back and digging her nails into him. It had been too long since she had last made love, and even though she was so ready for him it felt as though he had entered a virgin. She threw her head back and groaned as his body sent a million nerves ripping across hers bringing her to an entirely new dimension of pleasure.

"Yes, oh yes, at last," she pulled him to her, "at last, we're one again."

He saw tears roll out from the outer corners her eyes and flow into her hair and kissed them dry before showering her face with a drizzle of feathery pecks.

Only when he felt her relax did he start slow and sensual movements alternating with rapid and urgent thrusts till he felt her body tense and convulse with her climax and then his too, as he released himself inside her.

Satiated, both physically and emotionally, they lay in each other's arms, once again at peace with themselves and the world.

"Amrita…" He softly spoke her name into her hair holding her in the circle of his arms.

She smiled and snuggled closer to him listening to the song of celebration in the dancing flames. Listening to the whisperings of the gentle breeze as it caressed their united bodies. Listening to the stars and the moon and the entire universe as they reminded her that as long as the skies existed they did too. Aakash was her sky, she had told him so a long time back, and only when he was with her was she truly alive.

"Hey?" Aakash woke her from her reverie, " I just saw a falling star."

"Did you make your wish?" she asked him.

"No, I saved it for you. Mine was just granted," he said, winking at her.

They lay silent, happy to be together. He looked for familiar configurations of the stars and pointed them out to her. Like a diligent student she studiously hung on to his every word. It wasn't long before he felt her hands caress him under the covers.

He loved their intimacy and smiled as he said, "You are one horny woman, Mrs. Sud."

"You are one sexy professor, Dr. Ahmed," She retorted back, kissing his cheek. "You lie back and enjoy, it is my turn to devour you." She said as she once again cast her magic on him.

"Only you could have this effect on me." He laughed huskily, quite surprised at how soon he desired her again.

She then gave a whole new dimension to their pleasure. Her movements were sensual even to his eyes. Her hair laced his body with a whispering softness that seemed to be the antitheses to the wild abandon her body was causing to his. And then he was in the chasm, deep inside her, with the two of them riding the magical waves of their unique sensations. Her breasts rhythmically touched his chest as the two of them performed the tandem dance of passion to the music of the stars. At its peak, when the music reached its crescendo he held her hip as he pushed himself deep into her and burst several times in repeated thrusts.

Completely spent they lay content in each other's arms.

"What would the girls think if they saw me like this?" she thought aloud.

"That they need to learn a trick or two from you?"

"Funny," she replied.

"Well the first thing they'd have to learn is to respect your privacy. Then they'd have to learn to be less judgemental. At face value this would look so shallow, but you and I know better."

"So now what?" she asked him, as she rolled away to face the sky.

"Sorry?"

"I'll go back to India and you'll continue your life

here. Right?" she asked.

"We have little choice," he said kissing her forehead, "still it is what we choose to make it."

He was hoping she'd tell him this meant more to her than just a sexual release, that she was really in love with him too. He did not want her to give up her wealth, status and life for him. Just say that she loved him still like she did before, 'till the skies existed' *because they do Amrita, the skies still exist.* But she said nothing of the sort and he didn't push her. This was just another episode of sexual encounter in their virtual relationship. That's all.

She too thought about what he said and replied, "I'll be returning to India and you will continue with your life here. We may or may never meet like this again, who knows. You may find a steady and that would be wonderful. I would never do a 'Monica' on you, that's for sure."

"Come here Jaan," he pulled her in his arms again. "Let's take each day as it comes. Ok? What were those lines? 'Tomorrow will bring more lies', right? So is this the truth then?"

"'This is one truth," she replied honestly.

"'The day you change that sentence to 'this is the most important truth', you stop living a lie."

"It isn't that simple."

"It isn't."

"So now what?" she asked him again.

He smiled, "Nothing. A day at a time and we'll take it from there."

If she had any hopes that he would beg her to stay back or propose to her, they just went whirl pooling down the drain. She was a forty-year-old married woman with three children, why would he tie himself down with her? One thing was for sure that she would never tell him about Aasma, for he'd feel obliged to make a commitment then. 'A day at a time.' What a joke! How else did he think she had survived so many torturous years?

CHAPTER 28

It was almost daybreak by the time they arrived at the guesthouse. Amrita was surprised to find the lights on. Aakash had come to the door to see her in. Before her key could open the door it was opened for her.

Rhea looked disgustedly at her as she stepped aside to let her in. Then she dropped the bomb, "There was a call from home, Dad has been shifted to the hospital, he is in a bad way."

"Oh God! I have to leave immediately. When is the next flight out to Delhi, Aakash?" Amrita asked him.

"I'll find out for you," he said pushing his way past Rhea to the telephone. Amrita rushed to her room to freshen up and collect her passport and purse in the meantime.

"What are you doing here?" Aakash asked Rhea.

She had been violently sick at the high altitude, her body had been behaving strangely and she realized that she was pregnant. Ryan had brought her back home.

"What was she doing with you?" she questioned him back.

"Watch it, young lady, that is your mother you are talking about."

The line connected and that was the end of their conversation. "Later," he told her. "Hello yes, I need some information…"

"Amrita, you'd better hurry," he said aloud so she

could hear him from her room. "There's a Lufthansa flight in two hours from Baltimore. That's an hour's drive from here. We can make it. I've reserved your seat."

"Coming," she said running down the steps with her purse and jacket.

"Rhea darling, please pack my things and send it along with Aasma. Aakash, will you see to Aasma's return too please? Since the twins have exams she'll have to come back alone. Make sure she gets a direct flight, please."

"Don't worry Jaan, leave it to me. Let's go now." He said almost pushing her out to the car.

"Take care, Rhea. You look ill. Look after Alia; she needs you. Look after yourself. I love you darling," Amrita said as she ran to the car.

"Don't' worry about daddy, I'll be there soon to take care of him. Bye, give my love to the girls."

'No, this baby may not be yours and that is your punishment.' The words echoed inside her once again.

He was Aakash for her now and she Amrita. Jaan? Did he call her that? So late at night, where were they and what were they up to? Her mother was trying to steal Dr Ahmed from her, was she? Well, it was time to talk to him about a few things.

CHAPTER 29

It was too late. He was gone before she could get to the hospital. She broke down beside his body. Guilt got the better of her. It was because of her that he was struck by a stroke and now her meeting Aakash must be the reason he left her for good after hanging on for so many years. She was inconsolable. Not so much for the loss of a husband but for the fact that Rahul, even after his death, would stand as the invisible wall of guilt between Aakash and her. It was like he had played his trump card and beaten her at her game.

She called Aakash first and told him about Rahul's demise. Then she called the girls and broke the news to them personally. She requested Aakash to keep Aasma with the girls for two weeks and to send her back only after that. She did not want the child to suffer the rites and rituals that were customary after a Hindu death. The twins had exams; they must take them and do their best she told them. That is what their father would have wanted. She explained how he had left them ten years back, but now that he was released from his body would be with all of them at all times as their guardian angel. They would not be any closer to him here than they would be there.

Aakash had been wonderful with all three girls, easing their grief and just being a concerned friend. The girls went back to their dorm. They now shared a room together with Sarah.

Bobwana had been acquitted and Irfan was found guilty. Bobwana's parents took her back home. She needed more psychiatric help than Alia.

Aasma had been given special permission to stay with the twins in their room for two weeks. During the day she would spend her time with Aakash in the library. This was by special permission too. Aasma would generally help around, make his coffee and water the plants. Every now and again, when she wasn't busy, she'd become pensive and sad. So Aakash had given her library responsibilities to keep her comfortably occupied. They would discover new places to go to for lunch every day, and like him, she enjoyed Italian food the best. He encouraged her to talk about life in Delhi with her father. The sooner she came to terms with his loss, the easier it would be for all of them, especially Amrita. They would crack jokes to make each other laugh and then chew their food with a similar smile on their lips, a smile with one corner of the lip curving down.

"Coffee for my Profdoc." She had brought it to his desk while he was working, balancing the cup carefully with both hands.

"Thank you Angel. Hmm this is perfect," he said taking a sip.

"You want to learn my trick?"

"Trick?"

"Trick. To make the perfect coffee."

"Oh I see. Why should I when you do such a delightful job?"

"I won't be here forever, you know," she said spontaneously and put a knife through his heart. First Amrita now her daughter, he thought.

"There must be a way to keep you with me forever," he said.

"Hmm, there is. You'll have to marry me, you know,"

she said innocently.

He broke into loud laughter.

"Will you marry me Angel?" he asked her in jest.

"Nope."

"No?" He feigned disappointment. "Why not?"

"I'm in love with someone else."

"Really?"

"Uhuh."

"And who's the lucky guy?"

She looked at him with a shy smile, "Tom Cruise."

He was so tickled that he went up to her and gave her an affectionate hug.

"Good choice Angel." He winked at her.

CHAPTER 30

Rhea had been busy with her exams but was looking for an opportune time to catch Aakash alone. She had been shocked to hear about his break up with Susan but delighted in her heart of hearts. She would strike now, when the iron was hot. He had probably dated her so very available mother on the rebound. Now with her out of the picture too, he would be able to appreciate Rhea fully. She was almost twenty years old herself, half his age, but that would be of little consequence to him once he experienced her exotic body combined with her sharp brain.

But first things first, she had to do something about her pregnancy. What a mess she had got herself into. Ryan and she had had a great relationship. He was wonderful to her. Witty and intelligent, indulgent yet firm and most of all he understood and respected her moods. But still, it was Dr Ahmed she wanted.

Ryan had been happy about the pregnancy. He loved her. He loved her family. He knew that Rhea was headstrong and that she had a temper and could be selfish too, but she was very caring towards those she loved and she had a unique zest for life. Also, that deep inside she was a very insecure woman craving love. He would give her all the love she wanted because he loved her dearly. He was so thrilled about the baby that he proposed they get married immediately.

Rhea had thought he would support her decision and help her with the abortion. She was too young, there were dreams to fulfil and there was no place for children in her life now or perhaps ever. They had had a heated argument and she had walked away.

Aakash dropped them all off at the hostel after a farewell meal for Aasma who was to leave soon. He had given Aasma a book that she was to carry for Amrita. Enough was enough, thought Rhea. Why couldn't he forget her mother? Perhaps it was time to set her plan in motion. So the following afternoon she arrived at his office on the dot of lunch hour, when activity at the library would be more relaxed.

She knocked at his door and sought permission to enter.

"Rhea? What a pleasant surprise, come in, come in." Aakash welcomed her. "Coffee?"

"No, thanks."

"Sandwiches?"

"No, thank you."

"How are the examinations going?" he asked, genuinely concerned, knowing how difficult it must be for the twins to walk straight into tests soon after the demise of their father.

"Not bad," she answered.

"You okay, Rhea? You look pale and strained."

"I'm alright," she replied curtly.

"Listen to me girl. I know you are a proud and strong girl, but losing a parent is tough. Coming to terms with it is even tougher. Why don't you visit the school counsellor? These guys are specialists trained to help one through difficult times. Shall I make the appointment for you?" he asked her.

"Er… no thank you, it isn't that."

"No?" he was surprised. "Then what is it? Is it one of

your sisters? How are they doing?" he asked.

"They are coping pretty well." How should she tell him what the trouble was?

"It has to be Amrita then." He deduced and got up from his chair and went to the French window. He continued, half talking to himself.

"I knew it was a bad decision to let her go alone. Having to deal with such a big loss and all alone at that. It wasn't my call. Poor girl." He went to the coffee percolator. "It is something to do with your mother, isn't it?" He did not give Rhea a chance to reply and carried on, "To dedicate one's life to a invalid spouse and then not be by his side at the very end – even though it wasn't intentional – that is something she will never forgive herself for."

"She didn't love him," Rhea said quietly.

"Pardon me?" Aakash turned around; he could not believe that she had said this.

"Let it be."

"No Rhea, what did you mean by that?"

"I'm sorry, I was very rude the other day when my mother and you …"

"Are you changing the subject?" he inquired, turning back to the percolator to pour himself a cupful.

"Not really, we're still talking about the same person – my mother," she said sarcastically.

She waited for him to say something but he kept busy with the coffee he was preparing.

"You have always wanted to know why I hate my mother so much, isn't it?" she said to him.

He brought his cup to the table and sat on his chair.

Giving her his undivided attention he said, "Yes."

"I saw how she worked her magic on you, so I have come to warn you. She isn't the saint or martyr she portrays herself to be. She's been around, has been going around even when dad was ok."

With that she started her narrative and did not stop till she came to its very end.

"...He was already shouting at her when I heard them and came to the door. The last sentence that she said to dad was 'No, this baby may not be yours and that is your punishment.'"

Aakash stopped breathing as realization hit him. The child they spoke about was none other than Aasma, and if it wasn't Rahul's, then Aasma was his child. Aasma was his child. Amrita had given birth to his child.

Rhea was still talking, "He hit her with a lamp and she fell unconscious, then he too fell to the ground. That's when I opened the door and ran to them. I have not forgiven her ever since. It was her affair and her illegitimate child that I lost my father to. Aasma was not at fault, but I could not love her. It was Alia's episode that opened my heart to Aasma. I owed Alia's life to her. I forgave her."

Good God, thought Aakash. I have to get to Amrita now. Aasma, where is she? I want to see the face of my beautiful daughter.

"This is the reason I came to warn you about that woman. You've had your fun, now dump her before she dumps you." Rhea completed her narrative.

He looked dumbstruck at her. " 'That woman' is your mother. How could you believe this of her? How could you think so low of her?"

"Don't believe me? Here, take a look at this." She pulled out Amrita's diary and gave it to him. "Read this.

I found it while packing her stuff. It is full of her passion for her lover."

"Amrita's diary? And you read it? You showed no respect for your mother's privacy?" he asked her completely disgusted.

"She doesn't deserve any. Can't you see how she betrayed my father? Because of her my father lived like a vegetable the rest of his life. We all had to pay the price for her lust. Can't you see that?" she asked him feeling frustrated. "How easy do you think it has been for me? I couldn't tell anyone. I had to protect Alia, she thinks the world of her mother and would have died too if I disillusioned her. I did the best I could. That night I lost both my parents. I became completely alone." She held her head in her hands and started sobbing.

He got up and came around to her. Each one of us carries baggage, he thought. Amrita's was heavy and so was this child's. She really had too much to cope with and at a much more tender age. Aakash had seen his parents die and theoretically so had she. His heart went out to her.

"Rhea," he said and put his hand on her shoulder.

She got up and threw her hands around his shoulder and buried her face in his neck.

Aakash was taken by surprise; he did not know how to put distance between them especially with her still crying.

"And that woman," Rhea continued as she clung to him, "she had the audacity to spin her web on you." She had stopped crying now and was whispering her words. He could feel her hot breath through his shirt. "She saw how special we were to each other but she still made herself available to you. That bitch! That whore!"

He pushed her away from him with one powerful jerk and

then slapped her hard across her face.

She stood stunned holding her hurting cheek with one hand and covered her mouth with the other with tears streaming down her cheeks. Aakash was furious at the insults she threw at Amrita.

"Never," he pointed his finger at her, "never call your mother that."

"Understood?" he said to her in a very controlled but firm tone.

She looked at him in sheer disbelief and ran out of his office crying.

Completely stunned Aakash stood staring at the door that Rhea had just exited. His brain had far too much information to assimilate all at once and he just stood there in shock. Aasma was his daughter. His. His very own flesh and blood. His eyes were shining at the thought. On the other hand, Rhea was in love with him. Dear God! When and how did that happen? He walked out into the balcony hoping the fresh air would clear his spinning head and give him some clues.

Weren't she and Ryan…? Then how? To spite Amrita perhaps? Could it be? Oh Amrita, Amrita, where are you? Why haven't you answered my calls? What was that cryptic email telling me about your guilt and wanting to remain faithful to the memory of your dead husband? Which memories Amrita and what guilt? Haven't you punished yourself enough? You deserve to be loved Jaan, deserve to be loved.

You told me that you were walking out of my life so that I may find a woman who could love me completely. Amrita, you fill my soul in ways even I cannot comprehend. Can't you see that? God! You make me mad. Yes, I am angry with you. You've given me reason to be so.

Dear girl, you had my child against all odds; tell me, who can love me more than you do?

He opened her diary till he found the torn page and then holding it close against his heart he looked up at the skies with the same pain he had felt so many years back. His eyes implored the skies as every cell in his body cried her name out loud while his heart wept helplessly.

CHAPTER 31

"Rhea you have to talk to me. Why are you crying?" Alia asked her.

They were alone in the room. Aasma and Sarah had gone to the library.

"Leave me alone." Rhea replied.

"No, I think I know what it is and I will not keep quiet this time. You are pregnant aren't you?"

Rhea looked up in disbelief, "How did you know?"

"I saw Ulfat go through the same thing, I know the signs now. Ryan, isn't it?"

"Of course, what do you think I am?"

"Did he tell you to abort the baby too?" Alai asked in a stone like voice.

"No, he asked me to marry him. He's thrilled. I want to abort it."

Alia's face lit up. She had expected him to react the same way as Irfan had and was so very scared for her sister. She knew Rhea was capable of far worse than Ulfat.

"But that's wonderful. Marry him Rhea, he's a wonderful guy."

"Are you out of your mind? I'm in love with Dr Ahmed. Marriage, baby, these have no place in my life. I have to get my degree and go back and save our business."

"Dr Ahmed? Dear God! And save the business from what? Mom's doing a fine job."

"Save it from her."

"What?"

"It isn't the pregnancy that's bothering me. It's…" She wasn't sure if she should tell Alia everything. Maybe she was old enough to understand now and would help her.

"Yes?"

"It's mother?"

"Mom?"

"Yes."

She went on to tell a very shocked Alia everything. Then finished with "I'm in love with Dr Ahmed, he's fond of me too. But he's besotted by mom now, she's spoilt my life yet again."

"Jesus! Rhea what's wrong with you?" Alia shook her by the shoulders. "You heard a part of a conversation and based the entire blame on her? Did you ever open your eyes to see how devoted she was to dad? She was the one who kept him alive. She had no life other than him and us and you cast doubts on her? Gosh Rhea you should have spoken to me. Why didn't you open up to me at least? Why did you presume I would be weak? You presumed too much, that's the problem. You were too young and confused and you let that confusion stay with you till today."

She came and sat close to Rhea and wiped the tears off Rhea's cheeks with her hand. "I may not be as strong as you but I'm not weak, Rhea. I too have rules that I live by and one of them is to live and let live. You saw the negative side to Dad's stroke and I learnt to fight all odds and survive. I learnt from Mom that love could be a damn good reason to live. She came here for me and Dad passed away. How do you think that made me feel? But again I did not let guilt get me down. Everything in life happens for a damn good reason. Aasma came into our lives to save me, don't you think? Ulfat did not die for nothing; she gave me the strength to – save you perhaps. Maybe when mom came here dad was finally free to let go. Maybe something told him that mom too needed to be free again, that she would be all right and that it was time for them both to move on. Give her a reason to live, Rhea, you aren't the only one with the right to love."

Rhea listened to her sister like they were words from a messiah. She realized the trap that she was stuck in, a trap of her own making. Alia was opening the locks to all the doors she had shut herself behind. She realized she hadn't protected Alia as she had intended to instead she had harmed herself and those who loved her too. Her mother loved her; her mother actually loved them all, including her. *Oh mom,* she sobbed, *then what was it that I heard? Why were you punishing dad? Who's baby were you talking about?*

Alia had walked to the door and then turned around, " Love? You don't know the L of love. You're right; Dr Ahmed is only 'fond' of you. It's love, not being in love. Don't confuse the two. He loves me too and Aasma most of all, hate us for we are your competition, Rhea.' In love with Dr Ahmed.'" She mocked her sister. "Poor Ryan, open your eyes and see how much in love that guy is with you. Why Rhea, he loves you knowing your strengths and weaknesses. Now that is something. And what you have growing inside you is a part of him too. You made love, yes? Or was it plain lust? Think about it. The life in you is a product of sacred love. Yes, you have a right to choose, but he's helping you to make a decision you won't regret later. And the business Rhea? Take my share too." She opened the door to walk out.

"Alia," Rhea called out.

Alia turned to see Rhea beckoning her with her arms wide open. She ran back to her sister and they hugged and cried together.

CHAPTER 32

"Mom." Aasma came running out of the terminal to hug her.

"Aasma, my baby." Amrita hugged her. "I missed you."

"Me too. Are you ok mom?" She asked with tears welling up seeing Amrita look so pulled down in a matter of two weeks.

"I'll be ok now that I have my Aasma with me." She replied, fighting back her own.

"Not only Aasma mom, I have a surprise for you. See?" She pointed to the same exit she had just emerged from and out walked both Alia and Rhea.

"Oh my God." Amrita was so happy she started crying even before they reached her.

"Daddy…" Alia could manage only one word before she broke down.

They hugged and wept together oblivious of the onlookers.

"Mom, I'm so sorry," Rhea cried. "I've been cruel to you. I'm so sorry. I love you too mom, I love you too."

"I love you, my darlings, I always have and always will. You are all that I have and ever want." She told them all. "A mother's love is unconditional, you are my life Rhea, and don't you ever forget that. Let's go home."

"Wait, mom," Rhea said and turned around to look for that familiar face.

"Hello Amrita."

"Aakash?"

CHAPTER 33

"There's a Dr Ahmed come to meet you, ma'am, but he doesn't have an appointment." Her secretary's voice crackled over the intercom.

Aakash? Amrita's heart skipped a beat. For so many lonely years she had fantasized him walking into her office, this should have felt like a dream come true. Only now she wanted to put as much distance between them as she could. She had told him so although in not so many words. So why did he now travel the distance and walk straight into her territory? What did he want? She had to be on guard, she had to know.

"Please allow him to enter," Amrita answered, "and hold all calls and appointments."

"Mrs Sud." Aakash was escorted into her office. "What an impressive organization you run."

"What are you doing here, Aakash?"

"Ask me to sit down, offer me a coffee, where are your manners, girl?"

She called for two double espressos on the intercom while he made himself comfortable on the lounge chair.

"What are you doing here, Aakash?" she asked him again.

"In your office?"

"In my life."

"But I've always been in your life Amrita, haven't I?"

"I don't know what you are talking about."

"You do, but you don't want to admit it."

"That's not true."

"Not only will you not admit it to me but you are lying to yourself too Amrita."

"Whatever gave you the idea?"

"So you don't love me?" he asked her.

"Love? You should know better than that."

"No Amrita, I don't know what it is about love that I should know and not know. I have only learnt to suffer it. So tell me please."

A knock on the door broke the conversation. The coffee arrived, the bearer served them both and then left them alone again. Aakash, very appreciatively, inhaled the deep and satisfying aroma of the coffee liquor giving Amrita a few precious seconds to formulate her thoughts.

"Love is sacrifice, Aakash. Love is to give the others a chance to live," she said softly.

"And when do you start living, Amrita?"

"I have my life, make yours, Aakash."

"My life is being held ransom."

"By whom?"

"You."

"Me?"

"Yes."

"How?"

He finished the espresso shot with one swift gulp, put the cup on the coffee table in front of him and looked her in the eyes. "You'll know the answer to that the day you make yourself the single most important truth in your life. Everything will fall into place then." He stood up. "Good-bye Amrita."

For a long time she stared at the door through which he had walked out. Once again he had walked in and then out of her life. 'Good-bye Amrita' – walked out for the last time perhaps. The image stayed with her as she retired for the night. Sorely missing her diary, she opened a fresh one and penned her thoughts into it.

Love. Love is sacrifice. Love is giving those you love a chance to live. Love is to set free. 'I must learn to love with no hold.' Love hurts.

WHEN YOU GO AWAY.

When you go away …
The air around me will hold
your spell
And conjure you physically
there.
You wont' respond, there'll be
no bond
As I cry for you in vain,
Only I will feel the pain.

When you go away…
Nature will do as it deigns,
Life will dance and prance
around me,
Dawn will come again,
Light will break through the
shackles of the night,
Only I will feel the pain.

When you go away …
Every step will have to carry
The heavy weight of a broken heart,
Faces and places, names and games
A new life will start.
Only I will feel the pain.

When you go away …
Sing, dance, laugh, be happy.
Keep the sad tear from your eyes.
For if you cry, I'll surely die
Such heights my love's attained,
Even I will feel the pain.

CHAPTER 34

Rhea and Amrita were sitting in the den at their home. The same room that had witnessed Amrita's conversations with Aakash and then the dreadful fall out between her and Rahul. Rhea told Amrita what she had experienced that fateful night and Amrita wanted to kill herself for putting her child through such trauma.

But Rhea reassured her, "Mom, everything happens for a good reason. I was too young to know what dad was up to or how he hurt you in so many ways. I now appreciate your commitment to us. I also understand your affair perhaps. Most of all I understand why it was important for you to keep your baby. You could have lied to Dad, how would he know, but you were honest to all of us, including the man you loved, when you told Dad the truth."

Amrita's eyes welled up and the tears rolled out. Her baby had become a woman.

"I love Aasma, mom. I can't imagine life without her."

"Thank you darling, I feel like a heavy weight has been lifted off my chest. Like I have been forgiven. I can breathe again."

"Mom, a sin is forgiven and yours was no sin, I know how much you loved him and continue to do so."

"How's that?" she asked her daughter.

Rhea hesitated. She knew she was asking for trouble but she wasn't going to deceive her mother any more.

"Your diary, mom, what beautiful poetry you write."

"My diary." Amrita sat up. "You read it?"

"I'm sorry, mom." Rhea was ashamed. "But it moved me even then. Lucky guy."

"Where's my diary Rhea?"

"You'll kill me."

"I'll consider that if you don't return it."

"I don't have it with me right now, I'll send it to you when I go back." She replied guiltily.

"OK." Amrita conceded. The diary was a small thing compared to Rhea's love.

"Dr Ahmed had come to the office today." She wanted Rhea to know that, lest someone mentioned it to her by mistake and she misconstrue it.

"Dr Ahmed? You should have asked him for your diary." Rhea said it on reflex without thinking and then cursed herself.

"What?"

"Actually mom, I was jealous of the attention he gave you and so to prove to him that you already had a lover, I showed him your diary."

"You did *what?*" Amrita was sitting at the edge of her seat not believing her ears.

"He was upset with me too for reading your personal diary, in fact he slapped me really hard when I abused you in front of him. I think he's in love with you mom."

"So he has the diary?" Amrita asked her, intentionally ignoring the last sentence.

"Yes mom, I left it in his office."

"How much does he know about our lives?"

"Everything."

Amrita sat back with a sigh.

"Sorry, mom. I've made too many mistakes." Rhea came and sat by Amrita's knees on the wooden floor.

"It's ok love, we all make our share of mistakes." She recalled Aakash's words.

"Mom, I've made another mistake," Rhea said putting her head on Amrita's knees.

Amrita put a hand on Rhea's head, "What is it Rhea, tell me, don't be afraid. I'll handle it."

"I'm pregnant, mom."

"Rhea?"

"Ryan and I. I…I wanted to get rid of it, but I couldn't mom. It's my baby, I couldn't harm it mom. I want my baby, mom." Rhea broke down.

"Ryan, does he know?"

"Yes, he wants to marry me. I'm waiting for your consent. I'll do what you tell me to."

"Are you in love with each other?"

"Madly."

"I'm glad to hear that. Rhea, marriage and children are life-altering experiences, very beautiful and trying at the same time. Demanding yet satisfying. Are you sure you want to make these commitments?"

"More than anything, mom. I've lived my life very selfishly. I'm tired of that. I need to give love, lots of love, and let myself be loved too. I want my own family. Yes mom, I'm ready, for every thing it takes – and gives."

"Oh Rhea, Rhea, Rhea." Amrita sat on the floor next to her daughter and hugged her. "You have become a woman. Congratulations darling, I'm so happy for you."

"Mom, you're the best. Thank you."

"The wedding, we'd better organize that soon." Amrita said wiping their tears.

"He's in India already. We're going for an Indian wedding. Since he has no relatives in India, we'll have the wedding in Jammu. Dr Ahmed will stand in for his parents who are too old to travel. That's the reason he came early with us, he had to organize his 'hideout' as he called it. Oh, I'm so excited."

Amrita sat shell-shocked.

CHAPTER 35

Aakash's country home was looking beautifully spruced up. Everything else remained the same, only the paint job was fresh and the orchards had been manicured. Old memories fought to make their presence felt but Amrita visited each room with the girls like she was seeing it for the first time. They had put up in a hotel while the boys stayed with him. Paul had accompanied Ryan as his best man. The living area and patio were decorated with local flowers and freshly plucked apples from the orchard; the effect was refreshingly stunning.

The ceremony was over and celebrations well on their way. The kids were pushing off to Gulmarg for their honeymoon and Paul, Alia and Aasma decided to join them too.

"What is your plan of action mom? Will you come with us as well?" Aasma asked Amrita.

"No dear," Amrita said, a trifle embarrassed, "I'll go to Vaishnav Devi and then go back to Delhi."

Aakash coughed like he had just choked on his champagne.

Amrita knew it was intentional and her cheeks felt hot as fire. She had been extremely careful not to show any familiarity with Aakash especially in front of the girls. Even otherwise she did not want him to think now that she was a widow she would be waiting to grab him at the first instance. To love is to let live. He deserved his freedom too. 'A day at a time' as he had put it.

"I'll take you," he volunteered.

"That's all right really, I don't want to put you out Dr Ahmed." She turned him down politely.

"No trouble, in fact I had promised a friend a long time back and that visit of mine is due too. It would give me immense pleasure to do the honours." He bowed like a gentleman.

"I give you permission to escort my mom." Aasma got up and curtsied.

"Thank you Angel, what would I do without you?" He bowed to her this time.

"I'm still going to marry Tom Cruise," she curtsied.

There was a collective outburst of laughter at Aasma's unexpected repartee. When the boys were done teasing Aakash about losing his touch, Amrita, gently but with firm finality let her decision be known.

"I am going to Vaishnav Devi alone. This is something I've always wanted to do. Dr. Ahmed your offer is extremely kind, but I'm afraid I cannot accept it. I hope you understand."

If Aakash felt slighted, he hid it well. "But of course Mrs Sud. I completely understand."

"Thank you." Amrita silently heaved a sigh of relief. Her girls before herself – it had to be so! She had to put distance between the two of them. She could not trust herself anymore. He didn't have to touch her; the heat from his body reached her from the adjacent room. He didn't even have to look at her; she felt completely exposed. He didn't have to speak a word; her heartbeat said it all.

Everyone was happily high and even Amrita began to

relax.

The kids were busy cooking lunch for them.

"Profdoc, you go sit with mom and don't come here till we call you." Aasma ordered him as she physically pushed him towards the balcony.

This was the chance moment that he had been hoping for ever since Amrita turned him down. It was now or never.

"She's got a lot of the Hitler thing from you," he said to Amrita as he took the chair next to hers.

Amrita smiled indulgently glad that the others were too far to hear them.

"Wonder what she got from her father?" he said quietly.

"Um…"

"Any more poetry Mrs Sud?"

"Aakash."

"Why drop the pretence Mrs Sud, you hide so well behind it."

She lowered her gaze; thank God her face was turned away from the others.

He quoted the lines:

> When the skies are the limit for the power of love,
> Thence we shall meet and till then my love,
> Live well your dreams, I move out of your way,
> If the skies survive – we'll meet someday.

"When the sky is the limit for the power of love Amrita? I've heard that somewhere? Hey, wasn't that me who said this when you shared my bed that night right there in that room? You do remember, don't you? And also how, right here, on this patio, you told me that you were mine? Yeah? Remember? Where is my Amrita, Mrs. Sud? What have you done with her?"

The tears broke through the boundaries of her eyes and fell on her hands. He wasn't done; in order to penetrate all the barriers that stood between them he had to completely break her.

"Why did you move out of my way? To let me live my dreams? You did not even know what my dreams were Amrita. Had you known, you would have realized that I could not have lived them without you."

Biting her quivering lips and absolutely on the verge of a breakdown she looked up at him. Eyes made contact and a million unspoken words were left unspoken.

"Look up." He pointed to the sky and she did. "Can you see something?"

'If the skies survive-we'll meet some day.' He quoted.

"The skies survived Amrita, but we didn't. Why?"

She got up and holding her sequined chiffon sari up with one hand, she covered her face with the other and ran through the living room and out of the house towards the orchards. Aakash ran after her, and then seeing the baffled and shocked looked of all present in the living room, he stopped. It was very important to him that the girls accept the way he felt about their mother and then accepted him too. He did not want to force himself on them.

For a moment there was an awkward silence, till everyone grasped what had transpired.

"Mom…" Aasma immediately started following her mother when Rhea caught her in time.

"No, Aasma." She stopped her sister and looked at

Aakash, "She has the right to love too. Go get her, Dr. Ahmed."

A very knowing and affectionate look passed between Rhea and Aakash.

"Go man go." Ryan encouraged.

In a minute Aakash was out of the house calling out to her like a crazed man.

She had her face against the same tree from which they had broken the apples and was crying hysterically. He put both his arms around her against the tree, locking her within them. His face nestled in her hair, caressing the nape of her neck with little kisses.

"She's your daughter Aakash, she's your daughter." Amrita cried into the tree.

"I love you Amrita."

"How much I wanted to tell you, but could not. I didn't want her to come in your way."

"I love you Amrita."

"To give birth to her was my decision. You had every right to make your own choices."

"I love you, Amrita."

"She was a living truth in my life and would have been your guilt. I could not let that happen. I could not…"

"I love you Amrita," he said and put his arm around her stomach. She turned around and put her arms around his neck.

"I love you," he said softly.

"Me too," she whispered.

"What's that?"

"I…" she buried her head deeper into his shoulders.

"I didn't hear you. Come on you can't be that shy, not after the way you made love to me." He smiled and coaxed her on with a kiss planted on her hair.

She smiled at the thought, then looked at him and spoke with all sincerity, "I love you Aakash, I never stopped loving you."

He kissed her full on the lips, "Jaan."

She smiled, her eyes beginning to glaze up.

"My beautiful Jaan. Now do you think you can do one more thing for me?"

She raised her eyebrows in question.

"Do you think you can go back in there and say the same thing in front of the kids?"

She knew this was important, for acknowledging her love in their presence was to proclaim it to the world. Her girls were mature enough to handle the truth and it was time now to stop testing the limits of the forgiving sky.

"I can."

This was all he wanted to hear.

There were plenty of hugs and tears all around. Amrita looked even prettier than before now that she had Aakash fussing all over and indulging her. The girls were so happy, for their mother deserved every bit of this happiness.

Aakash asked Rhea to join him for a minute. He took her to the room that Amrita had stayed in.

"I want to show you something," he said and opened the almirah.

One shelf contained some neatly folded woman's clothes and another an overnighter. There was a musty smell emanating from them, like they had been there for years. There was a sacred book wrapped in red muslin cloth on the top shelf.

On the inner surface of the almirah hung a framed poem written on a page torn out of a diary.

Aakash picked up the book and removed the cloth with great care to expose Amrita's diary. He opened it to where a page was torn out off it and left the rest for Rhea to put in place.

Her eyes scanned the diary and then went to the framed poem.

> Dearest Aakash,
>
> For as long as the river flows, I will love you
> But the river can dry up.
> For as long as the trees grow I will love you
> But trees are destructible.
> For as long as the birds sing, I will love you
> But birds too are mortal.
> For as long as the flowers bloom, I will love you
> But even buds perish.
> For as long as the sun shines, I will love you
> But the sun too gets eclipsed.
> So I will love you for as long as the skies exist,
> I will love you for as long Aakash.
>
> Your Jaanu,
> Amrita.

She looked incredulously at him. No wonder he called her mother 'Jaan'. No wonder he had slapped her to her senses when she had abused her mother. My goodness how long had they loved each other and how deeply, she thought. Then it struck her, 'Aasma', 'Aakash'. Of course, he was the father. Her mother was true to her love, and truer to them in fact than she was to her love. A new respect was born for Amrita in Rhea's heart.

"I pray my heart is as strong as my mother's and my love as pure."

She said to Aakash and hugged him.

Aasma was thrilled to bits. "You're not going to marry me Profdoc?" she teased Aakash.

"You were my first choice Angel but you turned me down remember? So I decided to marry your mom, she looks a lot like you." He whispered loud enough for everyone to hear.

Aasma came to him and hugged him, "Good choice Profdoc." She winked.

"I'm glad you approve, Angel." He bowed and she curtsied. Everyone was hysterical with laughter listening to them.

"But now what do I call you, Profdoc?" she asked him.

"How about Tom Cruise, my naughty Angel?" he replied lifting her in his arms and tickling her belly with his nose.

"No, no, never." She laughed.

Rhea went and hugged her mother, "How about Profdad?" she suggested.

"Hmm…no, I got it," Aasma said with a click of her finger. "Can you guess?" she asked them all.

"You tell us Angel," was the unanimous chorus.

"Daddyprofdoc. Howzzat?"

CHAPTER 36

18 YEARS LATER

Dearest Daddy,

Many, many happy returns of the day to you. I wish we were there to celebrate your birthday together but next month isn't too far away. I am looking forward to so many things. To meeting everyone, eating the apples right off the trees, soaking my feet in the river, but most of all to handing the baby to you both and then sleeping. Tara is a complete night bird. Even at 16 months she has mastered the art of torturing me.

Raoul and Radha are a handful too, but their nanny is so very good with them. They celebrate their seventh birthday next week. Raoul wants a 'big people's' fishing rod - just like Daada's – if you please. You won't believe what Radha wants – A PONY!

Paul is a sweetheart; I get served breakfast in bed for allowing him his night of rest. His business is doing well and got a mention in the Fortune Five Hundred as one of the fastest growing companies in the USA. Wow! I know.

My work is on hold, 'the joys of motherhood' remember? But the kids who need serious counseling come home. I guess I'll be working out of the house a while more as Tara and her needs grow. I don't mind actually, I love being 'mom'.

Save a large chunk of cake for me, I'm hungry as a horse these days – you think I'm pregnant again? Shudder!!!

Lots of love to mom and you. Once again a very Happy Birthday to you from Paul, Raoul, Radha, Tara and me.

Write back soon,

Always your daughter,

Alia.

"Jaanu, come here and read this," Aakash called from the study.

"Coming," Amrita climbed up the stairs to what was her bedroom when she had first come to the hideout.

The name had stuck on and was on the official address too. Her room was now Aakash's study, his favorite room. He prayed and he worked here.

The almirah with her clothes and bag held its pride of place as the only odd piece of old furniture amongst the several modern bookshelves and the mahogany table that used to be in his bedroom. The almirah became a symbolic part of the lives of everyone who knew Aakash's sentimental attachment to it.

When questioned by little Neil, Aakash had proudly told him a story about how, many, many years back, while they were all away, Cupid would come to their home every day and bless these garments. That was why love reigned so strong at The Hideout. That it was The Hideout that had beckoned them home and united Amrita and Aakash. Rhea and Ryan and much later Paul and Alia had got married here too.

'And the empty bag?' Neil had asked.

'It isn't empty, Neil,' he had replied. 'Even the Gods visit our home every day and fill the bag with hope, wisdom and strength. Open the bag anytime you need these son, and you will find them in abundance.'

Not only Neil, they all believed the story to be true and held the almirah in equal reverence.

'Come on Daada, you can keep the almirah in your room or any of the other rooms you've added to The Hideout, why here?' asked his curious mind.

'And confuse the Gods?'

'But God is God,' the seven year old had argued, 'He can find the almirah anywhere.'

'This room is special son; you see the angles had come to sleep here one night several years ago. That is when they blessed it. This is His favourite room too.

Amrita had aged gracefully, her hair showed several strands of gray mixed with her original black and was tied back in a neat bun. Fine lines at the corner of her eyes crinkled even more when she smiled and she smiled a lot now. She looked elegant as she climbed the stairs in her handloom blue and beige raw silk sari draped on her slim figure, with a plain off white shawl draped carelessly on one shoulder. Aakash carried the years well too; at sixty-one he cut a very enigmatic persona.

"Jaan," Aakash called out again.

"I'm here love, I'm here." She chided his impatience as she placed a hot glass of ginger tea in front of him and went and sat on the floor cushions by the slanting ceiling to floor glass panes.

Rain was pounding hard on them, which made visibility reasonably clear because of the volume of water flowing on it. The room, like the rest of the cottage, was cozy and warm with a small fire that danced to its own song.

"Hmm, just what I wanted, you're a mind reader

Jaanu." He said sipping the hot beverage. "Listen to this, it a mail from Alia."

He read it out proudly and then looked at Amrita to see her reaction.

"Pregnant again?" Amrita laughed.

"Must have taken after her mother in bed." Aakash teased her as he clicked on Rhea's mail.

"Stop it." She blushed.

"Ready for Rhea's letter?"

"Ready."

"Okay, here goes…"

> Dear Daada,
>
> Happy Birthday.
>
> May you live forever and ever and ever and a day.
>
> Sorry if I sound mushy but I'm overwhelmed. You celebrate your birthday the day you were born Daada, but I celebrate mine on several days. The day you slapped me in your office-Rhea was born that day. The day Alia woke me from my selfindulgence- Rhea was reborn. The day you showed me mom's almirah-Rhea was born one more time. The day Ryan held our Neil and kissed me-Rhea took a new birth. The day Neil called me 'mummy'- I think I died and went to heaven.
>
> I now know what being 'mom' is all about, but even now I am in awe of mom and all she braved.
>
> I celebrate life and each day. Today, though, is extra special, for today on your birthday, I am renaming Sud Industries. It shall henceforth be called NeilAasma Industries. Ask madam chairperson if she approves of the name? The other two shareholders loved it, particularly Alia.
>
> Neil has a few years of college to complete but he has shown interest in the business and I can't wait to

hand over.

Ryan is opening yet another gym and this time in Goa, wants the sun and the sand in his old age he says. More likely the beer and babes. I tease him.

We'll be there next month for your anniversary as we all do every year. I can't wait.

Have a wonderful day and get mom to cook the same biryani for you. Take care of mom and you.

Your daughter
Rhea.

This time he didn't look for Amrita's reaction; she was looking at his.

He silently reread the mail to himself and then took off his glasses to dry his eyes before turning to see his wife.

"Please tell her I approve. It is a beautiful name, very sensitively created," said Amrita.

"I always knew she could move a mountain if she wanted to, but to move me so..." Aakash left his sentence incomplete and shook his head in disbelief.

She was looking straight at him with a smile full of love and amusement.

"Ready for Aasma?" he returned her smile.

She nodded sipping the tea.

Dear Daddyprofdoc,

You'll never believe what happened today. I, Aasma Sud Ahmed, have won my first court case. I was defending an undergrad nineteen-year-old boy in a molestation case. Some women have no morals daddy; she accused him just to spite him. You should have seen me; I was like Alia didi in court today. I just spoke to Alia and gave her the credit and now she's demanding a treat- wants the three sisters to spend a week in Greece!! I've promised her a Big Mac if she comes to visit me in LA.

Do you know who the prosecutor was? None other than Anant Khanna – five years my senior and the best out going student from his batch. Aren't you proud of me? Actually daddy, I've dated Anant a couple of times. He's a nice guy, very nice guy, and good at his work too. It was awesome fighting against him in court.

I know you and mom are happy for me. I really missed mom when the jury gave their verdict. She would have cried with joy, you know how she is, and if I know you, you must be teary eyed too. Am I right? Hah! I knew it.

Mom told me something several years back and it kind of stayed with me. That the sky holds everyone within it, those in flesh and those in spirit too, and that since I was your very own 'Aasma', you would both always stay in a very special place in me. You know what the weird thing was? When the judge came to congratulate me I honestly felt it was mom and you shaking his hands and proudly accepting all the good wishes.

Thank mom and thank you, my daddyprofdoc, for giving me this special gift.

And dad, wish you a very, very happy birthday. Keep my cake in the deep freeze like always; I'm coming home next month. Just a tiny piece, ok? They make size '8' really small these days.

Love to mom. She knows that her Aasma too will love her for as long as the skies exist, for Aakash and Aasma are one.

Got to go now, I have a lot of champagne to drink. Anant has made reservations in a fancy French restaurant. 'Either ways we'll celebrate', he had said this morning.

Love you so much,

Your victorious attorney,

Angel.

P.S.: There's another reason I'm so happy today. Didn't you read it in the papers? Tom Cruise has divorced Penelope, he is a free man once again, Yahoo!!

P.P.S.: Anant says he isn't as upset about losing to me as he is about losing to Tom Cruise. Giggle –you think he likes me?

He read it out and then looked up. It was Amrita's turn to reach out for a tissue to wipe her damp eyes. How well they all knew her.

He smiled at her predictability. "It won't be long before Aasma brings her beau home. Our little girl is in love. Aasma and Anant."

"Anant-Aasma," She corrected. "The never ending sky."

"Very nice, it's almost providential."

Amrita's smile reached her eyes and her face was glowing with pride and joy for her youngest born.

Aakash removed his glasses and silently blessed all his children before switching off the laptop.

He collected his glass of tea and came and sat beside Amrita on the floor.

"Cheers Jaan. Your turn to wish me."

"Happy birthday Aakash."

"A dry birthday wish?" he mocked surprise.

She laughed softly as she kissed his cheek, "That's the thirty seventh time you've made me wish you since morning."

"Who's counting? I'm claiming my present now." He

said and pulled her down so she was now reclining against the pillows.

"Still not counting, Dr. Ahmed?"

"Still not counting, Mrs. Ahmed." He kissed her parted lips. "Still in love with me, Jaan?"

"You can't imagine how much."

"Try me."

"Aakash." She said dragging the last syllables and it sounded as if she had transported herself from his name and merged within it.

He knew his Amrita and waited for her thoughts to collect before they came flowing out of her. He looked lovingly into her face and smiled.

Aakash,
What bliss to call your
name
– and see you smile.
What bliss to reach out
– and actually touch you.
What bliss to want you
to hold me
– and melt into your arms.
What bliss to sleep
– and have you to keep
me warm
What bliss to wake up
– and find you sleeping
still.
What bliss to cry
-and have you wipe my
tears.
What bliss to laugh
– and hear your laughter
too.

What bliss to sing
– and have you give me the words.
What bliss to speak
– and hold you in rapt attention.
What bliss to cook
– and watch you devour the food.
What bliss to fast
– and have you starve with me.
What bliss to recite a poem
– and watch you cry.
My heaven begins and ends in you
My beloved,
You are my bliss.

"Oh Jaan." Aakash was overcome with gratitude. He wrapped his arms around her waist and turned to pull her over him.

"Like it?" she asked as she adjusted the pillows under his head and then folding her hand on his chest and rested her head on them.

"Love it."

"Your turn now"

"You're kidding, I'm not a poet, I am a historian. I do biographies."

"So don't your characters have any poetry in them?"

"No, but they have a lot of romance." He winked at her.

Amrita laughed and her body rocking in a gentle motion on top of him was creating sweet waves of pleasure through him.

"Come on, Aakash."

"Dying to, Jaan."

"I meant the poem."

"The poem. Okay, let me think."

"Hey I can't if you do that," he added. She was tracing circles on his chest. He put both his hands behind his head and said, "Remember that poem that you had written when you were at your lowest and very lonely? It touched me deeply. I wanted to rewrite your life there and then. This is what I want to say…

> The sun still sets – but dawn comes too.
> When darkness pervades – my love will shine through.
> Not a star lights the sky – because they shine in your eyes Amrita.
> Now I sit by my window and truly believe,
> That the sky is the limit for the power of love.

"Nice?" he asked her.

"Brilliant."

"Want more?"

"Oh, yes please."

"I'm feeling very inspired. Let's see." He turned over, so that now she rested on the pillow and he was partially on her.

He locked his eyes with hers and said:

> Time cannot alter the waves of this hour,
> Amrita is mine and I'm her Aakash.
> We've passed destiny's test of time,
> In flesh and in spirit will you always be mine?"

> "For as long as the skies exist, Aakash
> For as long as the skies exist.

He looked at her like he had never before. He looked at her for a long time, caressing her hair and stroking her cheeks. Then he rested his head on her shoulder, kissed her palm, placed it on his cheeks and just lay beside her.

She understood the sentiment; it was the way she often felt when he held her close to his heart. It was the overwhelming feeling of gratitude to the Almighty.

She cradled him in her arms, carelessly playing with his hair with one hand and caressing his arm with the other. The pounding rain had been replaced by the soft drumming of light drizzle on the windowpane. The mountains were visible once again. He sighed and closed his eyes when she kissed his hair. They lay together, at peace with themselves and the world.

Dear Diary,

I've often wondered what course my life would have taken had Aakash not been in it.

Oh, how I love him so. He's more than a father to the girls; he's their best friend – and mine too. He's the reason I want to live another day and he's the reason I'll die content. What games does fate play! Who would have ever imagined that I'd find my Aakash, my piece of the sky, under such unusual circumstances? What would life have been had I met him before I married Rahul? … No. It's all clear to me now. Rahul was important in my life. He taught me a lot about marriage and love – everything it should not be. Had I not experienced that, I would never appreciate or love Aakash the way I do. Rhea and Alia, so close to my heart, I would happily seek the footprints I left behind in order to be their mother again. And Aasma's too - my miracle baby. My children were instrumental in bringing him to me. Fate, you do spin a conspiratorial yarn! I won't even try to understand you. Yes God, you did have one brilliant master plan for me. Thank you.

What was the verse I had written about love and God? Ah, yes!

What is life if not deep friendship?
What is friendship if not sweet love?
What is love if not a journey
To know there's a God above?

And God will come to me one day,
Take me back to life with Him.
The consummation of life will then be complete,
And my 'Ode To Love' begin.

Yes, I have found my Aakash, my piece of heaven, my love, my God.

My life is an Ode to Love.